RITUALS AND ROADTRIPS

MT EDEN WITCHES BOOK THREE

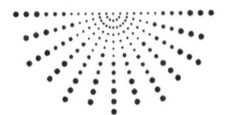

JAMIE SANDS

GREY KELPIE STUDIO

CONTENTS

ISBN

Kindle 978-1-7385967-3-7

Epub 978-1-7385967-4-4

Print on demand 978-1-7385967-5-1

Cover by Jacqueline Sweet

Note: there is a glossary of terms in the back of the book as I've used more Te
Reo and kiwi slang than usual

MT EDEN WITCHES BOOKS READING ORDER

Book one: Overdues and Occultism
Short story: Waiheke Christmas, available in the collected anthology Jingle Spells
Book two: Monsters and Manuscripts
Book three: Rituals and Roadtrips

Young adult spinoff: Onesies and Ouijaboards

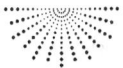

CHAPTER ONE

*B*asil brought out his luggage, blinking in the bright morning sunshine.

"Okay, if you're bringing those as well as the duffel, I'm gonna have to repack the boot." Sebastian pulled the tartan print suitcase out from the boot and set it on the driveway. That suitcase had all the clothes that Basil had packed for the trip.

"Yes, I am bringing them." Basil set the matching overnight bag and tote down beside Sebastian's feet.

"I'm sorry, I always overpack, it's a compulsion," Basil said. He shuffled his feet, then gasped. "I didn't get my cards or any crystals, or my book of shadows! Be right back."

Sebastian chuckled as Basil hurried back in through the open door of his Mt Eden villa and went to his altar. He wrapped his tarot deck in a handwoven cloth and placed his current favourite crystals in a purple velvet drawstring bag. He packed his book of shadows but decided against bringing his wand. He hadn't needed to use it much lately, his magic flowing freer and easier than it ever had before.

For the twentieth time that morning, he checked his pocket for the folded piece of paper that had their itinerary printed on it. Touching it soothed his nerves. He couldn't remember the last time he'd had a holiday, let alone a road trip with a boyfriend. Well, all right, he knew he'd *never* done that last one. He'd never had a serious boyfriend like Sebastian before.

It was all new territory and perfectly reasonable to be nervous about. His proclivity for overpacking was perhaps working overtime in the face of that nervousness, but Basil wanted to be prepared for anything.

He stashed his magical tools into a canvas tote Sebastian had bought him that read 'Can't even think straight' and pulled out the itinerary to look over it again. That day they would drive the two hours and twenty-four minutes to the small town of Waitomo. They would stay two nights in the historic Waitomo Caves Hotel, and then drive to Napier, staying a week before returning home. Pleasant, easy, and should be fun. Sebastian was keen to film some ghost hunts and there were a lot of accounts of hauntings at the Waitomo Caves Hotel.

Basil had rather enjoyed researching the history of the place. He carefully folded the paper and slipped it back into his pocket. He did a quick sweep of the small house, looking for things that might have been missed, and found Sebastian's toothbrush lying on the bathroom sink, waiting to be packed. He picked it up and went back out to the car.

"You forgot your toothbrush."

Sebastian, a light sweat on his forehead from loading their baggage, looked up and shrugged one shoulder. "I could've got another one."

"You don't need to though."

Sebastian stepped back and gestured at the boot of his car. The bags were neatly stacked in, arranged Tetris-style with no gaps or wasted space. "What do you think?"

"Very well done." Basil slipped the toothbrush into the outer pocket of Sebastian's laptop bag.

"Okay, is that everything now?"

"I, yes, I think so." Basil placed the bag with his magic things into the back seat of the car, to keep them handy. He pointed out the paper bag beside them to Sebastian. "Lisbet made us some sandwiches. She dropped them around while you were showering."

"Aw, that's sweet of her," Sebastian said. "Ready to go?"

"I'll lock the house up and then we can go," Basil said. He spoke softly to the charms on the front door to ensure no one but Judith or Lisbet would be allowed in. The charms hummed in a comforting way. Before he closed and locked the door he called out,

"We're going now, Eek! Judith and Lisbet will be coming around to leave food out for you once a day!"

A shuffling noise came from the ceiling, which was more or less how their resident house monster communicated.

Basil smiled at the empty hallway and locked the door behind him. He felt like Frodo Baggins, stepping out of the door and on the way to an unknown adventure.

But, he reminded himself, it wasn't unknown at all. He had the itinerary.

Sebastian, his handsome boyfriend, was behind the wheel of his hybrid SUV, sunglasses on and the engine already running. Basil slid in on the passenger side, secured his seat belt and clapped his hands twice.

"I'm ready, let's go!"

Sebastian leaned over and planted a kiss on Basil's cheek before he pulled out into the street. They'd decided to leave mid-morning on a Tuesday to minimise traffic. Rush hour was over now, and the streets were relatively quiet. Basil watched the familiar streets of Mt Eden pass by outside the car window and bit his lip.

Sebastian put his warm hand on Basil's knee.

"You okay?"

"Yes, of course," Basil said. "I'm just… it's been a long time since I took this long off work. Do you think they'll be all right?"

"Yeah, Lisbet's in charge, she'll keep everyone in line." Sebastian took his hand back as he turned them towards the nearest motorway on-ramp. "They'll be fine."

"I suppose so," Basil said. "And Sadie and Florence said they'd run the witch community group at the library in the evening, so that's ... I'll miss them, but it's good."

Mt Eden was behind them now, and they navigated the big intersections onto the Greenlane roundabout. Basil hated driving on these intersections and was extra pleased that Sebastian had offered to do most of the driving. The lights changed and Sebastian drove them neatly to the on-ramp.

"Some time away might be the best thing for you," Sebastian said. "Blow out the cobwebs, get you out of your rut."

"I don't have a rut," Basil said, stung. "I have a routine, and it's fine."

"I didn't mean it like that." Sebastian squeezed his knee again. Basil turned to look at him, observing a wide smile, totally at ease. "I meant, some new experiences might be good for you."

"Maybe."

"Think of those books you keep putting out for the shy kids, about going on adventures?"

Basil couldn't stop a giggle from escaping. "I was thinking about Frodo Baggins and stepping out the door, earlier."

"There you go."

The Southern motorway out of Auckland proper wasn't very interesting to look at, lots of signs for exits and suburban houses behind protective fences. He breathed out and pulled out the itinerary to read it over.

The itinerary was the same as the last time he'd looked at it. Soothed, he folded it again, slipped it back into his pocket and leaned back against the headrest.

Everything had gone all right so far, he'd remembered his magic supplies and the traffic wasn't too bad. He had his itinerary, so why couldn't he relax?

CHAPTER TWO

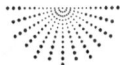

*T*ension drained from Sebastian's shoulders as they left Auckland behind. It was a beautiful day for driving, a clear late winter Tuesday with barely any wind and the roads opening ahead of him. He had put on a chill alternative folk music playlist on the stereo, and he felt at one with his car, with the road, with the universe.

But as the road wore on he became aware that beside him, Basil wasn't so relaxed. In fact, he emanated nervous tension that threatened Sebastian's chill.

"Look at that," Sebastian said. They'd begun the incline up the Bombay Hills and the landscape had opened out into farmland. "Sheep."

Basil chuckled. "Wow, sheep in New Zealand, that's a rare sight."

Sebastian counted the dry remark as a win. "Well, you didn't see sheep yesterday, did you?"

"No, I didn't." Basil's body relaxed.

Sebastian felt the tension lifting.

"I used to play this game with my parents when we went on a road trip where you had to spot horses. If you saw one horse it was one point, and three horses in one paddock is ten points."

Basil smiled. "Cute. Did you want to play it today?"

"We don't have to," Sebastian said. "But it's kinda fun. Oh, and if you see a goat, you get all the points off the other players."

"Why? What's so important about goats?"

Sebastian considered. "I'm not sure. I think it's because goats are cool and kinda rare, so that was a way to change up the game."

Basil chuckled again. "All right, so it's the first person to see a horse, and you say horse when you see it?"

"Exactly."

The road wound South through farm and bushland. Sebastian could drive forever. Something in his bones loved the road, loved the gentle turns and switching to cruise control on the expressway.

The sky was blue and open, stretching above him and the road led to the horizon. Sebastian's heart was full, and he sang along to his playlist. After a few bars he sensed Basil watching him. He glanced over.

"What?"

"Nothing." Basil stretched his legs as far as they'd go in the footwell and gave him an affectionate look. "You have a nice voice. I like hearing you sing."

"If you want to hear me really sing, switch to the playlist called 'Taylor.'" Sebastian joked, not thinking Basil would do anything about it.

Basil picked up Sebastian's phone and scrolling through his music app.

"Taylor Swift?"

"What? The woman can write a song, don't judge me."

Basil made an 'mm' noise which may or may not have been judgmental.

Sebastian chuckled.

Basil didn't switch the playlist but he did keep on scrolling the music app. "You have a lot of playlists."

"Well, I drive a lot. Or, I used to, I guess. And I have one for every kind of mood."

"This one is just three songs by the same K-Pop band over and over and over."

Sebastian laughed. "Well, I really like those three songs and I wanted to hear them a lot when I made the playlist."

"What mood is that playlist for?"

Sebastian squeezed the steering wheel and thought back. "It was a 'wanting to kick ass' kind of mood. I suppose it's motivational."

"Well, now I'm curious."

The alt-folk song cut off and the stereo started playing the first of Sebastian's favourite three BTS songs. He couldn't stop himself humming the intro and slapping the steering wheel with the driving beat. His energy surged, it always did when ON came on, but this time it was married up with the road and his first road trip in months.

He could drive all the way down the North Island if he wanted to, take the passenger ferry and drive the entirety of the South Island as well. Heck, they could even do Stuart Island at the end, he'd never done it before after all...

He *wouldn't* do all that, he'd stick to the plan he'd made with Basil. But the fact was that he could. He had his car and the open road, and he could do anything.

"I've never listened to K-Pop before, it's quite good isn't it?" Basil said, breaking his reverie and making him laugh.

Basil's foot was tapping.

"Yeah, it's really good." He put his hand on Basil's knee and squeezed it. Then he put both hands back on the wheel and launched into the chorus of the song, grinning from ear to ear.

CHAPTER THREE

*T*he drive had been pleasant enough, Basil enjoyed how much Sebastian seemed at home. When Basil had asked to stop for a toilet break, Sebastian had known the nicest, cleanest option for a public toilet on the route.

When Basil had mentioned he was getting peckish, Sebastian found a rest stop with a view over a river and they'd eaten Lisbet's sandwiches and watched ducks swimming past.

All the same, he was glad when the road signs started counting down the distance to Waitomo.

They'd driven through a lot of relatively flat farmlands, winding this way and that around the property lines, demarcated by endless wire and wood fences, and watched by numerous sheep and cows.

The landscape as they got closer to Waitomo was lusher, greener, with fewer imported trees and more native shrubs. They climbed a hill and then they were in Waitomo proper, welcomed by a sign and everything. The township was small, and the streets wound up and down hills.

Basil spotted a tiny piece of a bright white building, peeking out from between a stand of trees. "Is that the hotel?"

By the time he'd said it, the road had turned and it was out of sight again. A moment later they had a different angle and Basil pointed. The street they were on had several newer houses, but over those roofs, there was a dip into a forested valley and Basil saw a different part of the hotel. A prominent, three-storied manor apparently in the centre of the forest. The road approaching it was entirely obscured and it jutted out almost like the prow of a ship, with the green vegetation in place of the ocean.

Sebastian turned a corner.

"I think we're about to see the full thing…"

Suddenly the beautiful old Waitomo Caves Hotel was in front of them. An English country house, a manor almost, plonked in the middle of the tree ferns and other native trees. Basil's breath caught. It looked like the most haunted building he had ever seen.

The windows were old, their buckling glass reflecting the afternoon sunlight. The hotel's exterior was painted white but it was grubby in places, the trellising holding up bare climbing rose vines. The grand building overlooked the valley like an English lord, claiming land which wasn't his to begin with. It was large too, the part nearest the bank seemed like a manor, while the rest of the building looked more intentionally hotel-ish - with a grand entrance and a circular driveway around a patch of lawn with a flagpole spearing towards the sky.

Basil's skin prickled with goosebumps. Was it his imagination or was there something supernatural in the air? He sensed something…

"Look at it," Basil breathed. "Spectacular, isn't it?"

"It really is."

They pulled in under a white-painted wood and concrete weather canopy.

Sebastian put the car into park. "Not too many other cars, I wonder how many other people are staying?"

"I hope it's not just us," Basil said. "That'd be sad, and rather eerie given the size of the place."

They stepped out of the car. Basil moaned softly as he

stretched out his legs. The air was fresh, cool and scented with damp bark and trees.

Sebastian locked the car. "Let's check in."

They walked in together. The lobby wasn't as large as one might have expected from outside, but it was impressive all the same. To the right was an old wooden desk, possibly Kauri, definitely antique. On the left double doors opened to a generously sized dining room. The rear of the foyer was taken up by a large wooden staircase that hugged the wall as it ascended, starting on the right then using the back wall and turning left at the next floor. Floors and stairs were carpeted in a maroon-red. A collection of mismatched antique chairs sat around a small coffee table which held the day's newspaper, and the walls were painted a warm cream colour. It was absolutely delightful. Basil itched to take a seat on one of those chairs, pick up the paper and have a cup of tea.

"Welcome to the Waitomo Caves Hotel." The woman working at the desk gave them a bright smile. "How can I help?"

"Thank you, we're checking in. Booked under Black, Sebastian," Sebastian said.

The woman tapped on the computer. "Here you are, we have you for two nights, is that right?"

"That's right."

"Now, you have your pick of rooms. We only have two other guests checked in, so if you have any room preferences, I can probably accommodate them."

Basil pulled his attention from the charming decor and turned to listen.

Sebastian's eyes lit up and his expression turned sly "Really? Is 12a available?"

"12a?" Basil asked. "Is that different to twelve?"

The woman smiled indulgently. "Yes, they called it 12a because they didn't want to label a room with unlucky thirteen when the building was added on. It's available."

"That room please." Sebastian slid his credit card over the counter. "This is my boyfriend Basil, we were hoping to see some apparitions and I read that 12a is the most haunted room."

"It is," the woman said. While the machine processed Sebastian's card, she turned to Basil. "I'm Christine. It's lovely to meet you both."

"You too," Basil's hand twitched. He wanted to shake her hand but the counter in the way made it awkward.

She turned and retrieved a heavy iron key from a rack behind her. "We still use old school room keys here, still. And there's just one, so you'll have to share."

"That's fine," Sebastian said. "Thank you. Can we get dinner here tonight?"

"Of course. The dining room's open from five, and the bar is open now, they do some things like, chips and cheese nachos. Now, the Wi-Fi is sort of patchy here. We don't get a lot of reception, but the password's on this." She slipped a typed A4 sheet of paper towards them. "Along with the hotel rules and so on. Like I said, it's pretty quiet. Are you planning on doing the caves? We can book you in from here, if you are."

"Yes, we are," Sebastian said.

Basil picked up the key and his magic stirred in response. This key had *history*. The key had a sense memory of every hand that had touched it over the years, going back right to 1928 when the extension had been added. He breathed out mindfully and weighed the key in his palm. He hadn't known that the extension had been added in 1928 until he'd held the key.

He glanced up at Christine, but she was pointing out the door and telling Sebastian to park anywhere to the left. Neither of them had noticed anything. He took another careful, intentional breath and let his magic settle back down. Interesting that the key itself could have so much to say already. He got the feeling if he meditated over the key it would tell him a lot more.

Basil took hold of the mundane plastic keyring with the number 12a emblazoned on it instead.

"Thank you so much," Sebastian said. "And yeah, those two cave tours tomorrow would be perfect."

"No worries, you'll need to be at the information centre at 10:30, it's just down the road, I'll give you a map." She pulled a map off a pad of them and handed it over. "Your guide will meet you there."

Sebastian led the way back to the car, unlocking it and popping the boot. They unpacked their things.

Once the bags and cases were all out, Sebastian moved the car to one of the free parks on the left. Basil was picking up some bags when Christine came out to help.

"Oh, there's really no need, we're all right."

She brushed him off with a smile.

"We don't have a lift, so these all need to go up the stairs. It's all good, part of the service."

The three of them lugged the bags up to room 12a, up the staircase under the impressive gallery of framed Goldie prints portraying Māori elders, and through an arch to the corridor of rooms. 12a was close to the stairs, on the right-hand side.

Christine set the bags down just as the ding of the bell rang in reception. "I'll leave you to it, you know where I am if you need anything."

"Thanks, Christine," Sebastian said.

Basil stepped up to unlock the door. "Why you'd want to choose the most haunted room in the place is beyond me."

"Well, I could hardly risk someone else nabbing the room. What if something supernatural happened and I wouldn't be there to film it," Sebastian said. "Last time I was here there was a poltergeist in the downstairs dining space, but it's been banished now. I had to ensure we have the best chance of a sighting."

Basil fitted the key into the lock and felt an instant frisson of magic shoot up his fingers. Goose pimples prickled his skin. A wave of sadness flooded him then was gone. He stepped back, leaving the key in the lock and cleared his throat.

"Is something happening?" Sebastian asked. "Should I get out my camera?" He already had his phone up, recording.

Basil glanced at the phone.

"There's memory here, something very sad. When I put the key in the lock I felt magic, something happening…I'm going to try looking with some magic and see if this room has an aura to it."

He would have preferred not being filmed while he did this but well, he had agreed to it many times before. The hesitation was probably because they were in a new place and the key's memory had taken him by surprise.

Basil took a deep breath and drew on the well of his magic, letting it flood his veins. He closed his eyes and set his intention to look with his second sight. On opening his eyes again he saw light coming from the gap at the bottom of the door. He turned to Sebastian, smiling as he was comforted by the familiar warm, golden aura that was Sebastian's colours. He used that strength to turn the key and push the door open.

Inside there was no one physically, or at least, no one living. He could see a shining aura, silvery blue, very similar colours to the ghost in the library, all those months ago. It was eerie to see in the daylight.

Basil cleared his throat and spoke. "Hello there, I'm Basil and this is Sebastian. We're planning to sleep in this room for a few nights and we don't mean to cause any trouble. If… if you'd like to leave this place, we can probably help you to move on, but really, we don't want any trouble. If you're alright with that, we'll come in now."

He didn't move, waiting for a response to his words, which had his magic behind them - something he hoped would make the spirit understand the truth in them, the respect he wished to convey.

The aura moved, the person shape distorting to make a beckoning gesture. Basil turned back to Sebastian and his phone. "Can you see that? I think it's beckoning us."

Sebastian shook his head. "No, I mean, I can feel that it's cold but I don't see anything."

"Pity, it's quite beautiful."

"Could you describe it to me and the viewers?"

"Like a silvery blue cloud, I suppose, in the centre of the room, oh, wait, it's moving back towards the bathroom now. It's an aura without a person inside, it probably needs a ritual to be able to take proper form. Maybe then the camera will pick it up, or maybe it's a daytime thing." Basil paused to send his magical feelers out and sense if the ghost had any malevolent intentions. He felt nothing but welcome. He bent to pick up his suitcase.

"Yes, it's definitely welcoming us in, we mustn't be rude and keep it waiting."

He moved into the room, Sebastian followed closely.

Basil watched as the aura faded from sight. He turned back to Sebastian. His aura was still vibrant. "I think it's gone for the moment."

"That was awesome," Sebastian said. "I'll do a piece to camera about who it could have been, there are a couple of options."

Basil blinked slowly. "There are?"

"Yeah." Sebastian lugged the last of the luggage inside and hastily unpacked his camera and tripod, making quick work of setting it up in the window so he could face into the last of the day's natural light. "I thought you did research on the history of this place?"

"I did," Basil said. "I learned about when it opened, who owned it and so on, I figured you'd do all the spooky stuff."

Sebastian grinned wide, his eyes sparkling with unfettered glee. "Oh yeah, I definitely have the spooky stuff."

CHAPTER FOUR

*S*ebastian set up his camera and positioned himself in front of it, moving on automatic as he puzzled out a way to combine magic and technology so that he could film the way Basil's second sight saw.

To do that he'd have to understand how magic worked, and he didn't. Could Basil explain it in a way he could translate into technology? Sebastian shook his head, laughing at himself. This wasn't the first time he'd pondered that particular problem. He was buzzing with excitement. He'd been right to choose room 12a — they'd been instantly rewarded with a sighting.

"Don't be too long," Basil said, from the bathroom. He was hanging up his toilet bag and checking around the mirror. For what? Sebastian didn't know. "I'm starting to feel peckish."

"Won't be long at all."

Sebastian checked the light once more, decided it was good enough and started recording.

"Hey there, SpectreWatchers, it's Sebastian coming to you from the Waitomo Caves Hotel. We're in room 12a. Now, you might notice I said 12a and not thirteen? That's because the superstitious people who built this place didn't want to put in room number thirteen. Doesn't seem to have avoided the bad luck though, because as the story goes, a Māori princess fell in love with a British soldier who was stationed at the fort that used to be on this land." He paused for dramatic emphasis, and to give himself a chance to breathe.

"In the dark of night she stole out of her own pā to visit him, but one of the British sentries shot her, thinking she was a warrior coming to do some sabotage. She died instantly, but rumour has it she still haunts the hotel, looking for her lover. That's the hotel at large, but this room in particular?"

Seasbtian gestured to his surroundings. "Well, in the thirties, a man went down to dinner at the hotel's restaurant and told people at the bar that he'd seen the princess. Those listening didn't think too much of it. Stories of hauntings are commonplace here, after all. Except that he went back to this very room and hanged himself. They found his body the next morning."

Movement caught Sebastian's eye. Basil watched him, looking stricken.

Sebastian tried to give him a warm smile, but the stories he was telling weren't warm at all.

"So both of those people *could* be the one we saw on the way into the room. But there are other possibilities too. Basil suggested we could help them move on, if they want to, but given the long history of the place, and the large population of Māori people in the area, it's my guess they've hung around throughout blessings and other rituals already. I'm happy to be proven wrong, but it's my hypothesis that the ghosts in the Waitomo Caves Hotel want to be here."

He clicked the remote and turned off the camera.

Basil slipped his arms around Sebastian's shoulders. "You really think that?"

"Well, I mean, there's no way we're the first people who've come to this place in the last hundred years and offered to do an exorcism."

Basil hummed. "The feeling I got from the spirit was rather

warm, nothing angry or threatening about it. That could have been because of how I addressed it, of course."

Sebastian leaned his head back on Basil's stomach, enjoying the warmth of him. The room was bitterly cold.

"Shall we go get dinner? Warm up?"

"Sounds delightful."

Sebastian headed downstairs. He'd decided to leave the camera where it was and focus on his boyfriend for the evening. Basil seemed rattled from the ghost stories of the hotel. Sebastian wanted this to be a pleasant holiday as well as an opportunity to film.

The dining hall was largley empty. There were a couple of people at the bar, and one man dining alone. Other than that the tables were set but unoccupied. One of Sebastian's private hopes for these episodes of his show was to drum up interest in the hotel, and hopefully boost the number of tourists He was certainly going to film the glow worm caves the next day. That should draw in those who were interested in natural wonders as well as the supernatural.

A young man in a waiter's uniform ushered them to a seat by the window. "Welcome. I hear you're staying a couple of nights," he said with an easy smile.

"Word travels fast." Sebastian joked. Before he sat, he turned to the waiter and offered his hand to shake. "I'm Sebastian, this is Basil."

The waiter shook his hand, his eyebrows shooting up. "Tane. Do you want to hear the specials?"

Sebastian took his seat as Basil nodded. "Please!"

"We have pork schnitzel with wild greens and dauphinoise potatoes," Tane said. "The fish is snapper with butter sauce and today's pasta is penne with roasted vegetable sauce."

Basil hummed with appreciation. He already had his menu open. "Oh dear, those all sound absolutely delicious."

Tane grinned. "They're good, but for what it's worth, I think the schnitzel is the way to go, assuming you eat meat that is. I'll give you some time to look over the menu. Did you want a drink to start?"

"A glass of your house white wine, thanks," Basil said.

Sebastian ordered a hard ginger beer. Tane left them to get the drinks, and he looked over the food options. Sebastian hadn't registered being hungry, but as he looked at the food options his stomach rumbled.

Tane returned, took their orders (Basil got the schnitzel, Sebastian the pasta) and left again.

Sebastian took Basil's hand where it rested on the table and threaded their fingers together.

"This is nice." Basil gazed at Sebastian in a way that made his heart flutter as if they'd just started dating, even after all this time. Sebastian beamed back and squeezed his hand.

"Right? The people here seem so nice, and the place has such history."

Basil's expression sobered, and he looked over towards the bar. "Do you think that's where that man in the thirties said he saw the ghost?"

"Has to be," Sebastian said. "There's only one bar."

Basil hummed. "It's strange. Whichever ghost it was they had such a sad story, but the spirit didn't feel upset at all, more curious."

Sebastian nodded. "We can try and open communications. Maybe do a séance or get out the ouija board and see if we can talk to them directly?"

"Perhaps. Not tonight though," Basil said. "I want to rest, as much as we can with a ghost in the room."

"Hey." Sebastian tugged lightly at his fingers so he'd meet his eyes, and gave him a wide smile. "We've slept perfectly fine with a monster in the house. I don't see why this should be too much different."

Basil chuckled and took a sip of his wine. "I suppose you're right. I hope Eek isn't feeling lonely."

"They'll be okay."

Tane brought over two plates of food and a basket of warm bread. "Here's your dinner, lads."

"Thanks," Sebastian said. Once Tane had set the plates down he caught his eye. "So, Tane, which of the cave tours are the best, in your opinion as a local?"

Tane chuckled. "You asked the right guy, I do tours some days of the week. It really depends how extreme you want to go. The river caving is really fun, but it's not for everyone, like if you're a bit of a fraidy cat."

Basil raised his hand. "I'm a fraidy cat. I don't want to do anything where I get in the water."

Tane laughed from the belly, and Sebastian did too. "Okay, so none of the rafting. You probably want the basic package then. One tour through the oldest cave and then Ruakuri."

"Ruakuri?" Sebastian searched his rusty Te Reo. "Two dogs?"

"S'right," Tane said. "Legend says a young warrior was attacked by two wild dogs and hunted them down to the entrance of the cave. He found something much bigger than a kennel though."

Sebastian chuckled. "That's awesome. Is it okay to film down there?"

"Yeah, of course." Tane refilled their water glasses. "The tour won't be too busy tomorrow. We don't have many booked, so you'll get lots of time with your guide, and you can ask whatever questions or just film the glow-worms."

"That's great, thank you so much."

"Better eat up before it gets cold. Give me a wave if you need anything, okay?"

"We will," Sebastian said. "Those *might* have even been the caves Christine booked us into but I'll double-check. Now, let's eat."

Basil picked up his knife and fork and dug in eagerly.

"You didn't have to wait, Baz," Sebastian said.

"It's only polite," Basil said. "This is delicious."

Sebastian took a bite of pasta and nodded his agreement. "That is really tasty."

"Oh, I hope they have dessert," Basil said.

CHAPTER FIVE

*T*he hotel room warmed up quickly with the in-room heater, and they watched some TV before heading to bed. Basil stretched out under the bed covers, relaxed and satiated. The dessert of an old-fashioned ice cream sundae with strawberry sauce, chopped nuts and a pink wafer had been the perfect finish to his delightful dinner. On all counts he felt positive about the holiday so far.

Sebastian fussed around the room, making sure all his camera batteries were charging in preparation for the cave tours the next day.

Finally, he climbed into bed beside Basil and they read a while before turning the light out to sleep.

At some point later in the night, Basil was woken by a loud thump.

He opened his eyes, looking around the room. He saw nothing out of the ordinary. Perhaps it was someone in one of the other hotel rooms?

But there were only a handful of other guests and there'd been no indication anyone was staying anywhere near room 12a…

The door rattled as if someone were trying to force the door open.

Basil stopped breathing and groped under the covers for Sebastian's hand.

"Whuuu?" Sebastian mumbled.

"Someone at the door. Can't you hear it?"

Sebastian's eyes flew open. "Ghost or person?"

"I don't know." Basil tried to squeeze Sebastian's hand but he was already slipping out of bed. Basil flailed, trying to drag him back into the bed. "Where are you going?"

Sebastian went to the door, utterly fearless, and looked through the ancient peephole. "No one there."

The door rattled again. Sebastian jumped back. "Oh shi-"

Basil felt a tiny thrill that something had actually frightened his usually unflappable boyfriend, but the larger part of him urged him out of bed. He moved behind Sebastian and took hold of the hem of his sleep shirt. "What should we do?"

"Beats me," Sebastian said. "Opening the door seems like a bad plan."

Footsteps moved away from their door and up the hall. A moment later, they heard the noise of the door rattling again but more distant.

"It's trying other doors," Basil said. "Strange."

"I'm setting up a night vision camera tomorrow night." Sebastian turned back and wrapped his arms around Basil. He yawned in Basil's ear. "But tonight? Let's go back to sleep."

Basil was surprised and relieved to hear this suggestion. Basil fell asleep wrapped in his warm and muscular boyfriend.

He was woken again some time later, when the room was still dark. He heard footsteps up and down the hallway again. Perhaps it was someone who had lost their way, trying to find their room?

He pulled out from Sebastian's arms, feeling sort of brave. He unlocked the door and pushed it open, looking out into the hallway. He could still hear the footsteps approaching him, but there was no one there.

No one alive anyway.

He summoned his magic power, activated his second sight and immediately wished he hadn't. The hallway walls dripped with unworldly ichor. There were more noises, howling and the sound of crying. Worst of all, a small boy in shorts, braces and shirt, clothes that might have been from the 1930s skipped up the hallway towards Basil. He wasn't making the steady, heavy footfalls Basil had heard though.

Heart fluttering, Basil pressed himself against the doorframe, trying to take in every detail of the boy, and the hall itself, knowing Sebastian would want a full report.

He focused on his breathing, trying not to have a panic attack. Sebastian. If he called him, he'd wake up. But he'd said he wanted to sleep tonight and get filming done tomorrow. Why had he gotten up to investigate when he had no plan and absolutely no courage?

Basil screwed his eyes shut and tried to switch off his second sight.

He had no idea how to do it.

Switching it on reliably was something he'd only recently got the hang of.

Usually, he didn't mind waiting until it faded naturally. This time he wanted more than anything to see a plain, ordinary hallway before he climbed back into bed.

"Come on, Basil, you can do this…" he muttered. "None of this is hurting you, you're surprised and unsettled, but you're fine. Calm down."

He took a deep breath that rattled his chest on the way in and whooshed out. Then another which came easier.

He opened his eyes. The ghostly boy was fading from sight. The hallway was mostly ordinary looking.

But there was movement at the end of the hall, where the staircase landing was. There hadn't been anything there before.

Basil leaned over to see it more clearly.

It was an ordinary person, ascending the stairs from this floor to the next. He looked like the man who had been eating dinner alone in the restaurant. He didn't look Basil's way, and when Basil tore his gaze back to the rest of the corridor, it was back to normal.

Basil didn't hesitate. He backed into the room, locked the door and climbed back into bed, pulling Sebastian's arms around him. He was so deeply asleep he didn't stir except to tighten his grip on Basil.

It took Basil some time to get back to sleep. There was absolutely no doubt that Waitomo Caves Hotel was haunted. Sebastian was going to be delighted. Basil shuddered at the memory of what he'd seen. If only it wasn't too late to change their reservation.

CHAPTER SIX

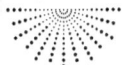

*S*unlight hit Sebastian's face from a gap in the curtains. They were on the wrong side of the building for direct sunlight, but the brightness was enough to wake him. His arm was partially numb from being pinned awkwardly under Basil, so he rolled closer and tried to adjust it.

Basil made a sleepy, annoyed noise, wrapping both his arms around Sebastian's arm. Sebastian melted with the cuteness of it all. He looked like a blond koala.

Just when he thought he couldn't be more endeared by his witch boyfriend, something like this happened. He closed his eyes and cuddled close, happy to put up with a numb arm.

He next woke when Basil stirred and rolled away, getting up to use the bathroom. Sebastian rubbed his arm until the numbness gave way to pins and needles. He sat back against the pillows and picked up his phone, scanning through the news feeds for anything possibly supernatural.

He found a small subreddit on the Napier locals thread about a car full of teenagers going missing on a trip out of town sparked his interest. He bookmarked the thread for checking back on. Probably nothing, but he wanted to know when the kids were found.

If he'd believed in religion he might have sent up a prayer for the missing teens, but of all the things Sebastian did believe in, God wasn't one of them. He believed in the universe though, so he sent out well wishes for the teens into the universe instead.

Basil came back into the room.

"This place is definitely haunted," he announced.

Sebastian put his phone down. "Is there something in the bathroom?"

"No, well, maybe. But I woke up at, well, I don't know, four a.m. or something. I could hear footsteps again, but there was no door rattling so I wasn't as scared. I got up and looked outside with my second sight and I saw all sorts of things, a little boy skipping down the hall and I suppose, ectoplasm? On the walls. Then a man went up the stairs, but I think he was the man from the dining hall and not a ghost."

Sebastian's eyes had been getting wider and wider. He bounced out of the bed in his excitement. "Really? You saw all that? I'll have to get you to do a recount on camera."

"Yes, of course, happy to. Breakfast first though, eh?"

"Yeah, breakfast sounds good."

Not long later they were both dressed and ready they went down to the restaurant for breakfast. The man from the night before was sitting at a table near the window, looking out at the garden as he sipped a cup of tea.

"That's him," Basil hissed in Sebastian's ear.

"I'm going to introduce myself," Sebastian said. Basil may have hissed a faint 'no' but he ignored it. He loved meeting new people, and if they were going to be some of the only occupants of the hotel it made sense to get to know each other.

The man looked up as Sebastian stopped at his table. He was

tall, thin and pale, with mouse-brown hair and bright eyes. He wore a checked button shirt and chinos.

"Good morning, I'm Sebastian Black, I'm staying a couple of nights with my boyfriend, Basil." He turned to glance at Basil who had held back, smiling nervously.

"It's a pleasure to make your acquaintance," the man said. "I'm Asher Montogomery." He reached out a hand and Sebastian shook it warmly. The man's hand was uncommonly dry and bony, as if he were far older than he appeared. Asher looked meaningfully behind Sebastian at Basil.

"Like I said," Sebastian said. "My boyfriend-"

"Basil Robinson." Basil came forward. He made no move to shake Asher's hand but nodded politely. "I believe I saw you on the stairs very early this morning."

"You most likely did," Asher said. "I apologise if I woke you, I suffer from terrible insomnia and sometimes walking around soothes me."

"Oh, no." Basil waved the suggestion away. "You didn't wake me, I was already… awakened."

Asher tilted his head with interest. "I expect the rumours of this place being haunted disturbed your sleep?"

Basil laughed nervously.

"Have you seen anything like that?" Sebastian said. "Ionly ask because I have a ghost hunting YouTube channel, and I'm hoping to do some filming for it while we're here."

Asher laughed, a sound as dry as his hands. "I don't hold with all that supernatural nonsense, myself."

"Right, of course," Sebastian said.

"We should probably sit down and order," Basil suggested.

Sebastian turned to see a waitress waiting nearby, menus in hand and a politely blank expression on her face.

"We'd better go. See you around, Asher, it was nice to meet you."

"And you too. I hope you enjoy your stay." Asher's smile didn't reach his eyes.

The waitress showed Sebastian and Basil to a table on the other side of the room. "I understand you two are doing the glow-worm cave this morning?" she said, as she handed each of them a menu.

"That's right," Sebastian said. "Looking forward to it."

"You'll want to take your camera, for your show," the waitress said. "Assuming you can film in low light. The glow-worms are beautiful enough but there's also some spiritual activity in the caves themselves."

Sebastian looked up, half expecting to see a teasing look. More often than not when he mentioned SpectreWatch people made fun of him, but she looked genuine.

"There is?"

"Yeah, you're doing Ruakuri. Ask your guide about it. They'll tell you the whole story."

"I will, thank you." Sebastian grinned, genuinely excited.

"What can I get for you?"

"Uhm, cappuccino and ah, the big breakfast for me." Sebastian's mouth was already watering at the thought of it.

"English breakfast tea and waffles for me, please, extra maple syrup," Basil said. "Thank you so much." She took the menus and went back into the kitchen.

Sebastian relaxed in his chair, feeling the day unfurl before him with a glorious promise of adventure and ghosts.

"It's cold," Basil said, for the thirteenth time. "I don't like it."

Sebastian pulled a black, knitted beanie with a rainbow flag patch on the front from his backpack and handed it to Basil. "Here, wear this."

He had pulled on his own cold weather jacket, a fleece-lined wind-breaker that always kept him pleasantly toasty. He hadn't thought he'd needed the beanie, he'd brought it in case. Basil's jacket wasn't really up to the bitter iciness of Waitomo. Sebastian made a mental note to visit an outdoors store at their next stop and buy something more hardy for Basil to wear.

They were waiting at the information centre for their guide to come and find them. Basil had insisted on being early, even though it was a brief walk down from the hotel.

The info centre also served as a gift and souvenir shop, so they browsed the shelves. Basil was looking through the books of Waitomo history. Sebastian was considering a small plush glow-worm toy that had a clip for fixing it to a bag.

"Basil Robinson and Sebastian Black?" Tane, their waiter from dinner the night before, called from the door. "Ready for your tour?"

"Absolutely." Sebastian hefted his camera. It was a small, portable model with decent low-light capabilities and followed Basil towards the door. Behind Tane stood Asher Montogomery, and two people Sebastian didn't recognise. A man and a woman, both blonde and blue-eyed, wearing brand new active-wear and knitted hats with "New Zealand" stitched into the pattern. Sebastian figured they were overseas tourists, possibly Swedish. Those hats were on sale at every souvenir shop in the country.

Tane checked a list on his clipboard. "Right, that's all of us. Follow me this way for the glow-worm cave, the first stop on this morning's tour. The first part is walking, then you'll have a boat ride."

Sebastian reached for Basil's hand and squeezed it, hoping he wasn't scared by the thought of the boat. Basil squeezed it back, he was smiling blandly, and there was no sign of concern.

The first part of the tour was mostly about appreciating the ancient lime caves, huge stalactites and stalagmites. Tane delivered a well-practised spiel, explaining the difference between the two and giving a bit of history. People had visited the caves as tourists since the time of the first European settlers, but they'd become especially popular after 1887 when some British men had done a survey.

"But the local iwi, we knew about these caves a good century or so before that," Tane said.

"Fascinating," said the male tourist. His accent confirmed that Sebastian had been right- they were Swedish. "Is there a prayer or blessing we can do while we're down there?"

"Thanks for asking." Tane seemed quite touched. "Just be as respectful as you can, that'll do. I'll do a proper karakia before we go into Ruakuri though, our second cave of the tour."

They stopped in a cave with an impressive floor-to-ceiling array of stalactites and stalagmites that connected in the middle. It was lit up, like much of the cave had been, with wall mounted lights, similar to an art gallery, designed to direct the light at the wall itself, not the room.

"No prizes for guessing why this formation is called the Pipe Organ," Tane said. "I'll give you a few minutes to take photos."

While Basil and the other tourists lined up to get photos of the beautiful rock formation, Sebastian approached Tane. "So um, any ghosts in these caves?"

Tane raised an eyebrow and gave him a cheeky smile. "Maybe."

"Like, should I start recording here or save it for Ruakuri?"

"Oh save it." Tane's expression sobered a bit. "There's definitely stuff in Ruakuri and you'll want to record the whole time there."

"Thanks, appreciate it."

"If you want to include me doing some of the history that'd be fine too," Tane said, off-handedly.

Sebastian grinned.

"I'd love to include you, always good to get local colour. I'll need you to sign a release form back at the hotel though."

"Fine, fine, could be my big break, eh?" Tane giggled and Sebastian chuckled

"Hey, you never know."

He filmed the cave. It was beautiful and good scene-setting for the video he was already planning in his head. He could show these images while he talked about their trip. He made a mental note to film the hotel's hallways and staircase as well.

The tour continued, taking them to a lower level of the caves. Basil stuck close to Sebastian. The Cathedral room was breathtaking.

"This is the cave with the highest ceiling," Tane said. "And it got its name from that and the shapes the rocks make over there." They looked up at the formations and hummed their agreement.

"Anyone want to have a sing? The acoustics in here are really good…"

Basil laughed nervously and shook his head.

Sebastian toyed with the idea but no one else seemed to be stepping up. He wasn't in the best voice, but he gamely raised his hand. "I could."

Basil's eyes widened. "You don't have to, Bastian."

"I know." Sebastian handed the camera to Basil. "But it'll be a cool experience. Never sang in an underground cathedral before. May as well film it."

"Good man." Tane clapped a warm hand on Sebastian's shoulder and directed him to a spot near the wall. "There's the best place."

Sebastian turned to look at the eager faces of their tour group. He felt the smallest wave of nervousness but it was overwhelmed by the novelty of the situation and his desire to create an awesome experience for all of them. The real challenge was deciding what to sing — BTS seemed rather out of place.

A childhood memory pushed to the forefront of his mind. He hummed a couple of bars, finding the note, and broke into a rendition of *Tutira mai nga iwi*

Tane beamed and joined in straight away, adding "Aue!" at the end of each line. Basil joined in after a moment as well. Basil's eyes never left Sebastian's face and he was beaming with affection and pride. Sebastian's chest flooded with warmth, so glad he could share this moment, this part of himself with his lover. He raised his voice louder, appreciating the resonance of the cave. The acoustics truly were amazing.

The Swedish tourists were filming on their phones. Sebastian smiled as he sang the classic Māori folk song about community and togetherness. He and Tane finished together, Tane bringing a low harmony to Sebastian's higher voice.

Tane, beaming, came in to give Sebastian a hongi, pressing their noses together and clasping hands.

"Thanks, bro. Usually people sing like, *Twinkle, Twinkle* or some top forty bs."

Sebastian was warmed by the gesture and surprisingly overwhelmed with emotions. He made a mental note to call his grandma the next time he had a moment. "You're welcome, of course, thanks for the tour."

The moment Tane moved away, Basil enclosed Sebastian with an enthusiastic hug that almost knocked him off his feet. "You're amazing. How did you do that?"

Sebastian chuckled. "I dunno, it's easy when you love the spotlight."

"More like the *lime* light." Tane hooked a thumb at the limestone surrounding them.

Basil groaned.

The Swedish tourists crowded in.

"That was beautiful, thank you!"

"Yes, thank you, that was truly special, do you mind if we upload the video to social media?"

"Not at all," Sebastian said. He pulled a business card out from his back pocket and handed it to them. "Those are my handles, if you want to tag me in your post, I'd really appreciate it."

"Thank you, we will!"

Asher Montgomery was behind them. He gave Sebastian an approving look. "Well done."

"Thank you." Flushed and happy, Sebastian took Basil's hand.

"Let's head down to the dock," Tane said. "On the boat, you'll get the best views of the glow-worms."

Once at the dock they all put on lifejackets and climbed into the boat.

Tane pushed them off with a large oar. "Obviously, don't stand up, don't rock the boat and don't lean too far. Basically, don't fall in the water. But also don't stand up because the ceiling gets pretty low."

The lights that had lit up the previous caves were missing from this part of the tour, but Tane shone a torch to reveal glow-worms hanging from the cave ceiling. They were bizarre-looking, almost outside of nature. Long strings hung down and formed eerie billowing swags, droplets of water clinging to them so they looked like strings of beads.

"The worms themselves are at the top of the string," Tane said. "They have glowing bottoms, the strings are to catch food."

"It's so beautiful," the Swedish woman said. "It's stunning." She took photo after photo with her camera.

Asher sat in the boat in front of Sebastian. He regarded the worms in silence, the dark obscuring his expression, his back ramrod straight.

Sebastian realised the man had barely said a word the entire tour. "How do you like it, Asher?"

"Mm, stunning, the way they turn a basic natural need into something so beautiful," he said. "Almost as if by magic."

Sebastian frowned. It was a weird phrasing. Did he know something he wasn't letting on?

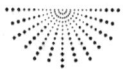

CHAPTER SEVEN

*B*asil wasn't as excited about the second cave as Sebastian seemed to be. Tane had explained in the drive from the first cave that it went very deep underground, which made Basil uncomfortable to begin with. On top of that were the promised ghosts, which he didn't really want to encounter with all these other people around.

To get there, they piled into a van and Tane drove them ten minutes from one cave to the next.

The original entrance to the cave was tapu, sacred, so had been closed off to the public. A huge winding spiral ramp was available instead.

Before they went in, Tane performed the karakia. The lilting tone of his voice as he chanted the prayer, filled the quiet valley. Basil felt the tingle of supernatural energy, like when they'd driven into Waitomo the day before.

They set off down the spiral ramp. The spirals were lit with footlights which glowed a warm, fireside orange. Despite the beauty, and the incredible design work that had gone into the structure, Basil felt more and more on edge with every step that led him deeper into the ground.

Halfway down, he realised the cause of his discomfort. His

magic was on alert, prickling at him, sounding a tiny warning alarm. Was it because of the sacred nature of the land they were walking on? Some sort of ancient magic from the local iwi that he was picking up on? Or was it the presence of ghosts in the caves below?

Basil looked around, rubbing the back of his neck. The other members of the tour group were chatting, The tourists nattering in Swedish, Tane and Sebastian discussing Sebastian's Māori heritage. Basil felt a pang of regret that he'd never asked Sebastian about it.

Counting heads, he swivelled, looking behind him to see Asher watching him steadily.

"All right?" Asher's forehead crinkled with concern. "Not getting dizzy are you?"

"No, nothing like that." Basil dropped his hand and tried to school his expression as Asher moved up to walk beside him. "I just… I suppose I don't much like being underground."

Asher hummed. "I think I know that feeling. A disconnection, isn't it? From the sunlight and the growing things."

Basil felt as if his innermost fear had been explained. "Exactly!" He smiled, feeling some tension release from his shoulders. "It doesn't feel like I *should* be down here."

"You'll be alright," Asher said. "We'll be out in the sunlight again in an hour."

The group came to a stop at the foot of the ramp.

Tane gestured up. "We've descended twenty-five metres into the ground. A distance like that isn't much when you're walking on the flat, but it hits a bit different going downwards, doesn't it? On this walk we're going to reach depths of up to sixty-five metres. That's about the same height as a twenty-storey building. Now, some of these caves were excavated by…"

The further they walked, the less Basil could pay attention to the words Tane was saying. The ancient magic of the caves thrummed around him. He looked this way and that, peering into the shadows, past the glow worms, to try and see evidence of it. Strain as he might, his eyes picked up only darkness.

He hurried to catch up to Sebastian and Tane. It wasn't polite to interrupt them so he tugged on Sebastian's shirt sleeve.

Sebastian turned instantly. In the dim light, his face was all angles and sharp shadows. Still handsome, but a little uncanny as well. "Basil, are you all right?"

"Yeah, I think... I can feel something." Basil dropped his voice to a soft whisper, but as the group had mostly fallen silent there seemed little point. They would be overheard.

"Everything okay?" Tane asked from the front of the group.

"Yes," Basil said. "I just, I sensed something. Silly really."

Tane chuckled, which wasn't exactly the reaction Basil had expected. "We're nearly at the part of the tunnel where the ghosts sometimes show themselves."

"Why is everything in Waitomo haunted?" Basil couldn't quite keep the whine out of his voice.

Tane's laugh echoed in the darkness. "Lots of history here. Once I was leading a group of tourists from Germany, I didn't say anything about the spirits, I stuck to the glowworm stuff, and one of the women caught my arm. She pointed up there." He directed his torch up, off the path, and illuminated a steep bank of lime formations, up to a spot near the ceiling of the cave. "She asked who the woman was."

Tane paused so that the group could respond. The Swedish tourists took photos of the spots, Sebastian directed his camera at it as well, and gave a shuddering laugh.

"A woman?"

"That's right. I asked her to tell me what she saw. She described a woman in traditional Māori dress, and as she did, she saw a man appear as well, dressed to go to war in a flax skirt, with full moko."

Basil's shiver started at the crown of his head and worked right down to his toes, prickling him with goosebumps. He blinked, tapping into the well of his magic to activate his second sight.

The magic of the caves responded, and when Basil looked up again, there they were. The man and the woman, both staring down with solemn expressions, both dressed in woven flax clothing, the woman with a feathered korowai over her shoulders and feathers in her hair. The man was dressed for war in a flax skirt that reached his knees. Basil's breath caught.

There was a gasp, followed by the click of a camera shutter, the Swedish tourists somehow still taking pictures while clutching one another.

Sebastian let out a pleased noise and moved right to the railing at the edge of the path, leaning to get a different shot. "Look at that."

Tane patted Basil on the back. "Well, there they are. The actual burial ground isn't part of our tour, that part is closed off, but every now and then one or both of these two appears."

He bowed his head and began to pray in Te Reo.

Sebastian glanced back at Tane, stopped filming and bowed his head as well. The others followed suit.

Basil glanced at Asher. He stared directly at Basil, not at the ghostly phenomenon.

Basil bowed his head as well, clasped his hands and willed his magic back down. He had no right summoning these spirits, although it had felt like they'd been there already, their presence at the edge of his supernatural awareness like a twinging elbow injury. He closed his eyes, breathed out slowly and as Tane finished the prayer, he opened his eyes to see that the spectres were still there.

They were fading, that was for sure, but still there. The woman met Basil's eyes with a stony expression and he felt guilty all over again.

He willed her to feel his regret at overstepping and looked away, respectfully.

After a moment, Sebastian lowered his camera and turned to Tane. "That was incredible, full-body apparitions!"

Tane nodded. "I'd be surprised if your photos or footage turn out though. Something about the cave or the spirits themselves… Every time someone thinks they've got a good shot of them, it never seems to come out right."

The tour moved on with a new atmosphere of excitement.

Basil couldn't shake the feeling that something was there with them, and that he didn't belong here. He was a descendant of colonisers after all, and he felt it acutely with every step.

At the deepest part of the cave, Tane guided them all to turn off their torches and phones, and experience the true darkness of being deep in the Earth.

Basil gripped Sebastian's hand.

One by one the lights flicked off. Tane guided them to hold the railing and walk forward. The place was full of glowworms, lighting up the blackness like stars.

Sebastian held Basil's hand. "It's so beautiful."

"There's a spot just ahead where you can look up through a natural chimney. It goes all the way to the surface," Tane said.

The group moved on, Basil trailed behind, trying to keep his heart rate under control and not panic about the thought of all that rock and earth between himself and fresh air.

Something grabbed his ankle.

Basil shrieked and jumped, losing his hold on Sebastian. His hip collided with the railing and he reached out, trying to find his boyfriend in the dark, breath coming in ragged rasps. His movement had dislodged whatever it was, but he was sure it would try again.

Tane switched on his powerful torch. "Everyone all right?"

Basil's eyes felt dazzled and he closed them again. "Sorry, it's only me. I thought something touched my ankle. Or, maybe grabbed hold of it."

Tane swept the beam of the torch back and forth along the walkway. "There's… the only animals down here are insects."

"Could it have been one of the spirits?" Sebastian slipped an arm around Basil, who instantly leaned against him, happy for his proximity.

"I'd be extremely surprised," Tane said. "They appear but they don't tend to interact in any way. That would be a first…"

Basil breathed out slowly, gathering his wits. The other tourists looked rattled, and who could blame them? He pasted a smile on. "Probably my imagination playing tricks on me. Sorry, everyone."

"Is everyone okay? Do we need to take a quick break, or shall we power on?"

"Power on," Sebastian said.

Asher made a noise of agreement. "Best we get out of here as soon as possible, if something is here."

Basil nodded in agreement and Tane led the way. They'd been at the lowest part of the cave, so the rest of the walk was a gentle incline. Basil wanted to enjoy the sights, appreciate the cave formations and the glow worms, but he was shaken and on alert. He stuck close to Sebastian, jumping at every unexpected noise.

They finally made their way back to the spiral ramp.

CHAPTER EIGHT

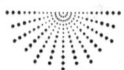

*S*ebastian carefully slipped his cameras into their bags and turned his full attention on Basil. "Okay, once more, tell me what happened?"

The rest of the tour group were dispersing. The Swedes climbed into their rental car. Tane chatted with Asher by the van that Tane had offered to drive them back to the hotel in.

Basil's eyes were flicking here and there, trying to track all the movement. Watching for something that didn't belong. Sebastian put his hand on his shoulder, trying to anchor him or reassure him that he wasn't alone.

"I felt the ghosts before I saw them, so I called up some magic, in case that was what they wanted," Basil said. "That was when everyone saw them. They formed physically I think with the nudge from my magic."

"Your magic allowed them to appear?"

"No," Basil said, quickly and decisively. "No, they didn't need my power at all, but I think it sort of prompted them, somehow?" He took a deep breath. "I didn't feel very welcome there, from the moment we started downwards. I don't think the spirits had any malicious intent, but I got the real feeling that I shouldn't be there, with my magic, doing things."

Sebastian frowned. Part of the Ruakuri caves were an ancient tribal burial ground, and although that part was closed off to tourists there were bound to be a lot of ghosts with certain views on intruders and colonisers. He rubbed Basil's shoulder. "And then in the dark?"

Basil shivered, moving closer to Sebastian, who automatically put his arms around him.

"Then it was like a horror movie. I felt a cold, clammy hand close around my ankle. That's when I screamed."

Sebastian's frown deepened. "We should ask Tane if anything like that's happened before. Because that sounds like something with nasty intentions."

"I didn't get a sense of what it was." Basil rested his forehead on Sebastian's shoulder. "Which now that I think about it, is weird. I can sense Eek in our house, and I can sense spirits fine. This was more like… absolute nothingness."

Sebastian squeezed Basil, not at all sure what to say to make it better.

Basil slowly relaxed as Sebastian rubbed his hand slowly up and down the back of his windbreaker. Finally Basil pulled away, pushed a hand through his hair and visibly pulled himself together.

"Ready?" Tane called out. He had his keys in his hand, jingling them. Asher had already taken the passenger seat in the front.

"Are we ready?" Sebastian searched Basil's face.

Basil had his colour back. He gave a thumbs up.

"Yeah, I'm dying for a cup of tea."

The van ride back to the hotel was quick and bumpy, and Sebastian resisted the urge to check his footage and instead concentrated on holding Basil's hand and reassuring him. But his mind was a whirl, trying out hypotheses for what could have touched Basil in the cave. He was also half planning how he would edit the footage he already had. He forced himself to think about the kinds of things that grabbed ankles.

He'd have to do some research.

It was early afternoon as they walked back into the hotel's grand entrance.

"How about we sit down in those armchairs in the lobby and have a cup of tea?" Basil said. "See if they have any cakes to go with them?"

However, the armchairs were already occupied by two Americans who were chatting loudly. Sebastian looked around.

"Tea and cake sounds good, who don't you grab a table in the dining room and order, and I'll drop off my gear in the room. Maybe get my laptop so I can start researching?"

Basi looked into the dining room while he tugged off the beanie to give to Sebastian. "Take that up for me? Oh and if you'd bring me my book, please?"

"Of course." Sebastian kissed his cheek and hurried up the stairs to swap things over.

When he got to the top of the stairs and turned, he was surprised to find the door to their room was open. For a split second his heart pounded with fear they'd been robbed, but then he saw the housekeeping cart was wedging the door open. Inside a woman in a tidy uniform was changing the bedsheets.

"Hi, excuse me," Sebastian said. "Can I get in for a moment? Just wanted to drop stuff off."

She looked up, a hand going to her chest. "Oh yeah, sure, let me…" She moved the cart back out into the hallway. "You startled me."

"Thanks." Sebastian went into the room and deposited his things onto the desk, then looked at the side table by Basil's side of the bed. There was a neat stack of half a dozen novels.

"His book, he says," he joked. "Which of the six do you think he means?"

The woman laughed uncertainly. "Maybe the top one?"

"Good thinking." Sebastian picked up the topmost book and was gratified to see it had a bookmark sticking out of it. "Thanks. I'm Sebastian by the way. We're here another night."

"Ngaire," the woman said. "How are you enjoying Waitomo?"

"It's great, we did the caves today," Sebastian said. Ngaire nodded, as if this was expected.

"We saw some ghosts down there."

She paused in her straightening of the sheets and glanced at him. "Did you?" Her tone gave away very little.

"Yeah, and weirder than that, my boyfriend felt something grab his leg. Have you ever heard of something like that happening down in Ruakuri?"

Now her expression turned into a deep frown. She patted the sheet down and straightened up. "No, that's unusual. People see spirits down there a fair bit, there's even a part of the path called the 'ghost walk' but I've never heard of anything grabbing. You sure he didn't imagine it?"

Sebastian hummed and shook his head. "I don't think so. He gets a bit jumpy, but I don't think he'd go that far… Well. I mean, from what I know of him. We've never been down a cave before, so maybe it was the new situation."

"The mind can play a lot of tricks down there. In all my life I've heard a lot of stories about that cave but never things that grab you."

"Interesting," Sebastian said. "Thanks, Ngaire. That's really good to know."

"No worries. Have a good stay."

"Thanks for doing up our room." Sebastian waved and retreated downstairs. Could Basil have imagined the touch?

Well of course he could have. But not with his extra senses, and heightened awareness of the paranormal. The mind could play tricks, and Basil was prone to getting nervous and panicky.Even so, Sebastian didn't think it was likely.

He walked down the stairs slowly, looking at the oil portraits on the walls and wondering who they all were.

When he re-entered the dining room , he saw Basil seated by the window with three books stacked in front of him and a fourth open. He had one elbow on the table, his cheek in his hand, leaning forward over the book, obviously deep in whatever was written there.

Amused, Sebastian plopped the novel he'd retrieved on top of the unopened books. The sudden noise broke Basil out of his concentration and he blinked up at Sebastian as if he'd forgotten who he was.

"Here I thought I was bringing you important reading material," Sebastian teased. He sat opposite Basil. "But you've found your own, like a book-sniffing bloodhound."

Basil chuckled. "I found a shelf. It's a lot of paperbacks people have left behind, holiday read kind of stuff, but these were in there too." He lifted the book he was reading, which was old with yellowed pages, the linen bound cover falling apart. It bore the embossed heading "Legends of Waitomo."

"That looks very relevant."

"It is," Basil said. "I'm going to ask if I can restore it."

"Restore it? Like take it back with us and fix it in the library?"

A waiter appeared with a tray of tea things and a plate of small cakes and slices. Sebastian moved the book stack to one side as they set the tea things on the table.

"No, I brought some things with me, just in case." Basil said it as if it were the most obvious thing in the world to have brought with him. Sebastian stifled a giggle.

"You're telling me that one of your bags has what, book glue? Some weights? Tape? So you're ready to restore a book at a moment's notice?"

"Excuse me, did you need anything else?" The waiter said. Basil looked at the things on the table and shook his head.

"This is perfect, thank you." The waiter left them to it.

"I can't believe you brought a book mending kit with you," Sebastian said.

Basil's cheeks pinked but he nodded. "You never know when you might need them. And look, it's already come in handy! I'll talk to Reception after we've had tea and make sure I'm not stepping on any toes."

Sebastian's heart swelled in his chest with affection for his boyfriend. "You're completely adorable. Ridiculous, but adorable."

Basil poured the tea, blushing even more.

Sebastian wanted to reach over and ruffle his hair but the table was too wide.

He set his laptop to one side and accepted the cup of milky tea Basil handed him. He took a sip and hummed. Basil always made his tea exactly as he liked it.

"Adorable," Sebastian said again. He let all his affection colour the word and was rewarded when the tips of Basil's ears turned rosy pink.

"Thank you."

Sebastian cut each cake and slice in half so that they could both have a taste of everything, which had become a habit with desserts and cakes in the last few months. For a time they didn't talk about much but how nice the sweets were.

Then Basil took a breath. "I'm going to see if I can find anything in these books about malevolent spirits or other reports of things reaching out."

Sebastian pulled his laptop closer. "I'll do the same online. Oh, and I spoke to the woman tidying our room and she said she'd never heard anything like it, although she'd heard lots of rumours about ghosts and things."

"Hmmm." Basil frowned and opened one of the other books up. "Well, let me know if you find anything."

The next half an hour passed in silence, Basil flipping pages and Sebastian's keyboard keys clicking quietly.

The local news sites were reporting on the missing car of teenagers now, just a couple of sentences, but it was spreading around.

Finally, Sebastian looked at the sparse notes he'd made on a Word document and closed the laptop. "There's nothing online about Waitomo except ghost sightings. Much like we had today, although varying numbers of spectres."

"And this book seems to imply that because of the tapu nature of the caves, there's nothing dangerous there unless you're desecrating graves. Which, well, we weren't."

Basil and Sebastian frowned at each other for a moment. Sebastian cleared his throat, uncertain about suggesting what he was about to.

"We could go down again, see if you attract it again?"

Basil drummed his fingers on the tabletop. "I don't much want to, but it does seem to be the only way to get an answer."

He stood up and picked up the book that needed repairs. "I'll talk to Reception now and see if they can get us on another tour."

Sebastian opened his laptop again, checking his feeds for anything strange, which was a habit he'd formed years ago, before even starting his YouTube channel. He almost did it on automatic.

The missing Napier teens had a brief update - no news at all. *Police baffled by car vanishing* was the headline. Sebastian chewed the inside of his cheek and hoped there'd be more news soon.

He sighed, closed the laptop and stretched his arms up over his head. If he wasn't careful his neck and shoulders would ache from hunching over his laptop. He idly wondered if there was any gym equipment at the hotel. Sebastian snorted. The Waitomo Caves Hotel didn't seem like that kind of place.

Basil returned and sat back down. "No problem, we're on the early tour tomorrow, nine-thirty."

"Perfect," Sebastian said. "And what did she say about the book?"

Basil beamed. "She was pleased, she wants me to do as many repairs on as many books as I can manage."

Sebastian chuckled. "Well, that's your afternoon sorted then. Did you want to do it down here or in the room?"

Basil considered this. "There's a bit more space down here, I think. I'll go and get my supplies. What are you going to do?"

Sebastian stretched his legs under the table. "I might have a wander around the hotel, see if I can find some good spots for filming tonight. Then I'll find us somewhere to have dinner."

"Perfect." Basil got up, kissed Sebastian on the forehead and hurried off the room.

While he was gone, Sebastian piled up the dishes to one side of the table. The waiter returned. "I'll take those. Will you be needing anything else?"

"I'm sure Basil would like the teapot filled again, please. He's going to be gluing books and things, I hope that's okay."

"I might just open a window," the waiter said thoughtfully. They cleared the dishes then returned to crack one of the nearby windows.

Sebastian was in the middle of clearing his own things off the table when Basil returned. "Oh, is that fresh tea? You read my mind."

"It's hardly mind-reading to guess my tea-loving boyfriend might like some English Breakfast." Sebastian stood up. "I'll be back in an hour or so."

"Thank you," Basil said. "See you soon, Bastian."

The hotel was a lot less spooky during the day, although the sunlight didn't exactly filter through to the hallways. Sebastian had stowed his laptop and picked up one of his smaller cameras, thinking he'd film some atmospheric shots and details that couldn't be picked up at night.

The hotel was large by rural New Zealand standards but exploring the common areas didn't take too long. He filmed the hallways the guest rooms were on, and the staircase, then snooped around on the ground floor.

He ran into the woman who had been cleaning his room as he took the back corridor behind the dining room, Ngaire.

"Can I help you find something?" she asked.

"Oh uh, I was doing some filming." Sebastian dug his card out of his pocket. "I have a ghost-hunting show and I read about a space back here called Cat Alley? Is that off limits, or could I…?"

Ngaire took his card and examined it. "Thanks. It's all right, the chefs are doing some prep work but dinner doesn't start for a while so you shouldn't be in anyone's way."

"Thank you, you're the best."

Ngaire led him through the door to the back area of the hotel. Although it wasn't exactly off-limits, it didn't feel like a normal space for guests. The carpets were more worn here, and there was only one faded picture on the wall. The rest was ageing wallpaper. She pointed out the door to the kitchens so that he'd know not to go through them, and left him to it.

Sebastian took a moment to set up a tripod in one corner where he could get a decent shot up the hallway. He took his EMF in his hand and with the camera rolling, made a thorough investigation of the hallway. He moved slowly, tapping gently on the walls and speaking in a low voice.

"Is anyone here with me? Are there any spirits here that'd like to make themselves known?"

At the farthest point from the camera, closest to the kitchen doors, something knocked back.

Sebastian stopped, looking around.

"Who's there? Can you rap again?" He tapped twice on the wall, paused and tapped once more.

After a few seconds the sound echoed back at him. Something or someone was tapping on the wall back to him.

He inhaled, grinned at the camera and gave it a thumbs up.

Beep beep beep

He looked at the EMF in his hand, which was showing massive amounts of information being received.

He cleared his throat. "Who's there?"

For the sake of ruling it out, he openeded the connecting doors to the corridor to check no one was on the other side of the wall messing with him. He switched on the go-pro on his chest as he did this, so that he could cut in footage that showed, as he suspected, there was no one around.

Of course, he didn't check the kitchen. There was a chance Ngaire had told the kitchen staff what he was doing and they were now pranking him, but Sebastian knew in his gut that wasn't the case.

He moved closer to the camera.

"This area is meant to be haunted by a little boy who died tragically of scalding. Reports from people who have seen him have indicated he's not a malevolent spirit, more like a kid who wants to play. Basil's account of seeing him in the hallway last night corroborated that. So, let's see if that's who we're dealing with here."

He went back to the wall, watching the EMF reader spike as he approached the same spot he'd heard the noise before. His heart was racing but he wasn't afraid, so much as elated. He hoped something more than just the noise would show up on the footage.

"Daniel? I think I read your name was Daniel, and that you like to play? Is that you there?"

No response.

If only I'd thought this through better, I could have brought a rubber ball or a teddy bear to something to lure him out with. Ah well, there is something I can do and I doubt he'll be able to resist it.

"Hey Daniel, can you finish this?" He tapped out the five beats of 'shave and a haircut' and left the last two beats to fate.

He waited. Long enough that he thought it hadn't worked, then distinctly and without doubt, the replying two taps resounded in the hallway.

Sebastian beamed at the camera. "Once again, for the naysayers." He tapped the first five beats again, and this time, a lot quicker, received the responding two taps.

Sebastian's EMF was beeping so insistently he turned it off. It was getting colder in the hallway.

"I think Daniel is joining me. The temperature has dropped noticeably here in a very short time."

A child's giggle right behind him.

He startled badly, dropping the EMF reader and spinning to face whatever was there.

He saw nothing.

If only Basil was there with him. Basil could see more than he could, could tap into his magic and see the paranormal planes. But it was too late for that, and he had to make the most of his time with Daniel while he could.

He straightened his spine, cleared his throat and ran a hand through his hair. "Hello Daniel. Nice to meet you, I'm Sebastian. Is there anything you'd like me to do? Anything that you need resolved?"

The giggle sounded again, from behind Sebastian *again* and he spun in place, laughing a little himself now. "Are we playing a game?"

The giggle again, as if Daniel were circling him, sticking behind him.

Sebastian paused, then turned as quickly as he could. "Ah ha!"

The giggle sounded louder than ever and seemed to skip backwards towards the wall.

They played like this for maybe thirty seconds, both of them laughing. Sebastian enjoying himself in a way he never had before on a ghost hunt.

Daniel seemed to tire of it soon though.

Sebastian stopped hearing his laughter. He licked his lips. "Daniel, are you still here with me?"

The faintest of tapping noises. This time it was on another wall, the one with the only picture in the corridor hung on it. The frame tugged down on the left-hand side. The picture was an artist's rendition of some tree ferns, and it looked as old as the building itself. Watercolours that had faded along with the wallpaper.

There was a faint giggle, and the corridor abruptly became warm again.

"I hope we got that on camera," Sebastian said. "But it seems like Daniel wanted to make the picture crooked before he left."

He approached the picture frame and took it in both hands to straighten up again. The wallpaper behind the frame wasn't as faded, so it was clear to see where it should be sitting.

On a whim, or perhaps, ghost hunting instinct, Sebastian gently lifted the framed painting and noticed the wallpaper had been tampered with. He set the painting down and ran his fingers over it. There were clear lines where someone had cut a rectangle out, then pasted it back down. Like a letter box opening.

Nothing in the world could stop Sebastian once he was curious. Making a mental note to pay for any damage he was about to make he picked at the corner of the pasted down piece of paper with a fingernail. The ancient paste crumbled to dust and the paper lifted off neatly in one piece. Behind it, a hole in the wall.

Before he went further, Sebastian stepped back, picked up his camera off the tripod so he could film this as he discovered it.

"Some kind of hidden nook here. I'm not too sure what's in it, but Daniel seemed to want me to know about it so let's see what's there."

Steadying the camera on his shoulder with one hand, he used the other to reach into the dark cubby.

He imagined spiders, cockroaches, and worse, creepy chilled hands grabbing his, but he was too invested to let fears overcome him. He reached in and touched something leathery. He pulled out a slim book, overstuffed with letters and pieces of paper.

"Will you look at that?"

Sebastian turned the book this way and that, showing it off to the camera. "I need to show this to Basil. And the people who run the hotel, more to the point. But what a find."

He switched off the camera, slipped the piece of wallpaper into the cubby and replaced the picture on the wall, packed up his things and went to show his prize to Basil.

CHAPTER NINE

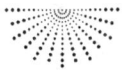

*B*asil was deep in book repair mode. The hotel staff had even brought him some paperweights and moved an extra table over to his so he had more space to work on the books.

They were old, fragile things, but with some of his own magic, and some industrial strength paper tape, he was reinforcing the bindings, repairing spines and reattaching covers that were hanging by a thread.

He was in his own world while he did this, humming softly to himself, probing with his magic to find the weakest spots, and reinforcing them with a dash of pure love. This was, he considered, what he was made for.

It was true that his magic could do a lot more than bind books, but he felt utterly at peace, utterly himself while he did this work.

When Sebastian said his name and tapped his shoulder, he almost jumped out of his skin. He had just finished gluing an old spine and weighting it. Sebastian had obviously been waiting for a safe moment, but it jolted Basil right out of his reverie.

"Sorry," Sebastian said hurriedly. "I didn't mean to startle you, but I have something you need to see."

Basil turned in his seat, one hand rubbing his chest where his heart was thumping and took a breath.

"Bastian, yes, sorry I was completely absorbed. What is it?"

"Okay well." Sebastian pulled a chair beside Basil's, then looked around. Basil hadn't realised it but a couple of the hotel's staff had been watching him for some time, and they tugged their chairs in closer as well.

"I hope it's not weird that we were watching," Christine said. Basil recognised her as the staff member who had checked them in the day before. "But I'd love to learn how to do all that book repair stuff and you're more interesting to watch than YouTube."

"I'm flattered," Basil said, faintly. "It's all in the glue and tape, really." Had they that he was using magic when he worked? If they had they didn't seem at all upset about it, so that was something.

"This is Ngaire," Christine said, indicating the other woman in a hotel service uniform. "She wants to learn as well."

Ngaire waved her fingers at him.

"A pleasure," Basil said. He turned to Sebastian, feeling as if he was still in a deep dream and nothing was quite making sense. "Sorry, what did you want to show me?"

"Right." Sebastian laid the book down on a clear bit of table. Basil, Ngaire and Christine all leaned in to look at the cover. "I just had an extended and interactive encounter with Daniel, the little boy who haunts Cat Alley, right over there."

"With a ghost? Oh the little boy? I saw him last night." Basil woke up a bit more, genuinely pleased for Sebastian. "Did you film it?"

"Yeah," Sebastian said.

"He's a scamp," Christine said, affectionately.

"We played a game and everything, it was incredible, I'm hoping the footage comes up well. Anyway, he tugged on a picture, and when I looked behind it, there was a little cubby hole. Well, there was a piece of wallpaper." Sebastian turned sheepishly towards Christine and Ngaire. "I'm sorry, but I just peeled it off, I was caught in the moment. I'll pay to repair it of course."

Christine chuckled. "I'll put it on your room bill."

"So what's this book then?"

Basil moved his things to one side and gently drew the book towards him. The cover was plain, blue linen bound with no title or author on the front. He opened the cover gently, aware of the dry glue on the spine and not wanting to damage it in any way.

Inside were yellowed pages filled with writing. The date at the top said April 4th, 1931 "A journal," he said. He flipped some more pages. "No, not only a journal, there's recipes and shopping lists in here too."

"Recipes?" Christine leaned over to look. "Oh, imagine if we got the kitchen to do vintage recipes, that might be a real tourist draw."

"So long as it's not tripe and hardtack," Sebastian said. "But other old-school stuff might be interesting."

"Indeed." Basil slowly flipped the pages, making sure not to damage anything although the paper seemed to be relatively well preserved. It must have been nice and dry inside the wall. "I wonder why Daniel wanted you to find this?"

"It's a bit of the history of the place," Sebastian said. "Perhaps he wanted to help out. No offence but this place isn't exactly bustling with tourists."

"No," Ngaire said. "Our off-season has spread to a lot of the year. People come to New Zealand to see Hobbiton now, and our caves feel like a second-best offering."

"But this could open up a good new direction for us, truly lean into the history of the hotel, and the ghosts and everything." Sebastian was getting more and more excited. Sebastian was even prettier when he was enthusiastic about something. Now he was positively radiant. Basil caught himself staring. He looked instead at Christine and Ngaire.

"Shouldn't we be setting the ghosts to rest, though? I mean, ghosts are usually here because of unfinished business and so on."

Ngaire frowned and shook her head. "Our spirits have chosen to remain."

Christine tapped a finger on the table. "I know what you're saying, Basil, but it comes from a certain, shall we say colonial standpoint. The local iwi, we believe that if there are apparitions they're usually here to communicate something with us, or to watch over us. They will come and go to the spirit realm as they choose. They have been mourned, so there's no sadness or anger attached to their appearance. There's no need to do any exorcisms or whatever."

Basil swallowed down his first reaction, which was to argue he wasn't a coloniser. He knew that was a knee-jerk reaction, not his true feelings. His family were, after all, predominantly white. He nodded instead and cleared his throat. "I see, yes, good."

"You saw that ghost in our room on the first night," Sebastian added. His expression was thoughtful. "But it hasn't caused any trouble or even made the room cold since then."

"That's true." Basil rubbed his arm. "It only felt serene there, easy to fall asleep. When I looked at the hallway with my second sight, there was a lot happening but it wasn't harming anyone. It didn't even respond to me, come to think of it."

Ngaire gave him a reassuring sort of smile. "We really appreciate you restoring these books."

Basil felt on firmer ground. "It's my pleasure. This journal probably just needs a bit of glueing around the spine and then it will be more robust as well. For what it's worth, I think your idea of using these recipes in the kitchen is a particularly good one. In terms of the spirits, do you mind if Sebastian and I are filming them for his YouTube channel?"

"Not at all," Christine said. "Chuck in some pretty shots of the outside of the hotel and we're golden."

"We'll make it look like a very great place to stay," Sebastian said. "I'll link to the website in the video description and everything."

"I suppose that means there's not really any need to head down into the caves again, after all." Basil felt inordinately pleased at this idea. "Because you already got footage of the apparitions."

Sebastian's eyebrows raised. "I guess not. I suppose the mystery is still whatever it was that grabbed you but we don't have to."

"It might have been a random magical event," Basil flapped his hand. "I really don't want to test it and see if it gets worse. Let's not go down there again."

Sebastian gave Basil a fond look. "Fine with me. The journal is an excellent find, I can round out the episode with that."

Christine and Ngaire carefully removed the books which were drying to store somewhere safe, and Sebastian went back to the room to review his footage.

Basil felt the niggle in the back of his head that said ghosts *had* to be put to rest, even though Ngaire had told him it wasn't so.

He flipped through the pages of the journal, and in the back found the time when the boy had died. There were a number of pages mourning the loss, and the horrible way he had died. It seemed he had been playing in the kitchen and upset a pan of scalding water over himself.

Daniel's mother, Rose, had copied out the police report, and detailed her fears of losing her job. Daniel hadn't meant to be in the kitchen at all, after all. But her manager had been sympathetic, and had given her paid time off to grieve, with her job secure.

Basil smiled faintly at the generosity of the long-ago man, and flipped the pages. The very last entry in the journal was tear stained, and Basil tensed as he read it.

The strangest thing happened today, as I was walking down Cat Alley, bussing plates from the restaurant, I heard my Daniel laughing.

I looked around and saw nothing, but plain as day I heard

*him. I put the plates in the sink as fast as I might and hurried back
into the alley in case he was still there. All at once I felt a
profound sense of joy. I haven't felt that since before the accident,
so I was rightfully startled, but again I heard Danny laugh and I
knew what it meant. He's still around. He's not angry at me for
not keeping him safe. In fact, I think he's keeping me safe now.*

*I clasped my hands and thanked heaven that my boy is all
right. Long may he stay in the alley to warm the hearts of the
visitors here.*

Well, that was conclusive. Basil dismissed the niggle, took a
photo of the page of the journal to show to Sebastian, and to look
back on, and let out his breath in a happy sigh. He relaxed into his
chair, and sank back into book repair mode. If they were leaving
in the morning, he had work to get finished.

CHAPTER TEN

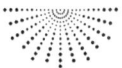

The next morning Sebastian woke up from a deep and satisfying sleep, feeling more refreshed than he had in a long time. He retrieved his camera from the spot he'd fixed it in the hallway to record timelapse overnight and uploaded all his footage from Waitomo to cloud storage for safe keeping.

Basil got up. They had a leisurely breakfast and then packed up the car to leave.

Sebastian made sure there was a copy of his card at reception and promised to let them know when the videos went up.

With Basil in the passenger seat, and the hotel behind them, Sebastian fell once more into his happy driving place. The roads wound as they made their way out of Waitomo, leaving behind the strangeness of the caves and the wonder of the hotel. What surprises did the rest of the trip hold for them?

They wound through the farmlands and countryside. It was a drizzly day, with grey skies. Sebastian queued up his more moody playlists to suit the weather.

"I hope we make good time." Basil looked at the hotel reservation documents he'd printed out. "They say reception closes six this evening, how long did you say it would take to get there?"

"It's less than four hours." Sebastian put a hand on Basil's thigh and squeezed. "We have heaps of time. Enough to stop in Taupo and get lunch somewhere nice, if you want to."

"Oh." Basil carefully folded the documents away. "That's all right then."

Sebastian put his hand back on the wheel as they approached a sharp corner. The farmland around them felt older than other parts of the country. Large boulders and jutting rocks pushed out of the grass here and there.

"Look at that, Baz." He pointed at a cluster of rocks that all appeared to be standing up. "Like the Aotearoa version of Stonehenge."

Basil made an amused noise that wasn't quite a laugh. "They do look peculiar don't they? As if tossed there by a giant."

Sebastian nodded, enjoying that image. "Do you want to stop and have a look?"

Basil turned his head as they drove past the stones, following them with his eyes. "Better not, they're private property after all. Besides, we need to get to Napier."

Sebastian bit his tongue. He wanted to remind Basil that they had plenty of time, but he suspected it wouldn't actually alleviate whatever anxiety he was feeling. He let it go and focused on the road instead.

As they drove through the Kinleith pine forest, on the outskirts of Taupo district, the car started doing something strange. It wasn't as responsive as usual, and there was an alarming sponginess to the brakes when he pressed them on sharp corners.

Sebastian frowned. "That's weird."

"What is?" Basil looked out the window, concerned and then back at Sebastian. "What's wrong?"

"The car's handling strangely." Sebastian checked the readings on the dash. "No idea why, plenty of petrol, the temperature's fine, it's just... strange."

"Oh stars." Basil wrung his hands together. "Should we pull over? I think I saw one of those rest stop signs, there might be a good place?"

"Let's get to Taupo. We can take it to a garage, get it checked out."

The drive to Taupo was tense, made more so by Basil quietly panicking beside him. At least he was staying as quiet as he could manage, but every time they hit an incline or a sharp corner, his inhales were audible, and his hand gripped the armrest of the door with white knuckles. He emanated tension.

Sebastian tried his level best to ignore him, and focus on the car, but the stress was contagious even so.

His heart raced, and his grip on the steering wheel was tight.

He watched the road, willing the car to keep it together until they could safely stop in Taupo.

The road seemed longer than it should have been.

Sebastian had driven this road a thousand times and he was sure it didn't take this long. Sweat beaded on his temple. He felt a growing suspicion that something was interfering with his car. Something supernatural.

"Are you *sure* we shouldn't pull in at a rest stop?" Basil's voice was unusually wheedling, a bit higher than normal.

"I can get us there, don't worry." Sebastian had already dropped his speed from the usual 100kph of the open road to a safer feeling eighty. Several cars and vans had overtaken him. Finally they turned a corner and the forest started to thin.

"There, we're almost there."

"It's just-"

"I said I'll get us there and I will." Sebastian snapped. He instantly regretted it. "Sorry, it's… I need to focus."

"Of course." Basil sounded cowed. Sebastian felt horrible, a bad boyfriend.

He swallowed his apology as another turn came up and the car braked so slowly his heart rate escalated again. He breathed a sigh of relief when the 50 sign appeared. Crawling into the township wasn't so bad. He pulled into the first mechanic he saw.

Turning the car off was a relief.

Basil sagged beside him.

Sebastian turned to him. "I'm sorry for snapping back there, but I really wanted to get the car somewhere we could get it looked at, and I knew I could do it safely."

Basil nodded, his face a picture of sorrow. "How will we get to Napier?"

"Let's see what the mechanics think, and then we'll work something out." He patted Basil's knee and then got out of the car.

The mechanic's was in a squat concrete building which was painted bright red, boasting 'Best Mechanic in Taupo' in yellow lettering. There were two open bay doors where a few people in coveralls were working on cars. The familiar smell of petrol and grease hit Sebastian's nose. He loved places like this. Car mechanics knew their business and they didn't mess around.

A young white guy with the name tag 'Gavin' sewn onto the chest of his coveralls came to meet him.

"Hey there," Sebastian said. "Not entirely sure what's happening, but the brakes started reacting weirdly about a half hour ago. Could you take a look?"

Gavin ran a hand through his hair, already looking at the car as if he wanted to dissect it. "Sure. Can look at it right now, take about an hour, probably."

Basil had climbed out of the car and was stretching his legs.

Sebastian handed Gavin the keys. "We'll go get some lunch I guess."

Gavin took his number, Sebastian grabbed his satchel which held his laptop and notes, Basil took a small bag which no doubt had some books in it, and they left the car in Gavin's hands.

The mechanic was a couple of blocks from the lakefront, so they walked in that direction. Sebastian knew the best places to eat were closest to the lake. "What sort of thing do you fancy for lunch?"

Basil hummed and tapped his chin. "I don't feel terribly hungry. Maybe just something light."

That rattled Sebastian even more than the business with the car. He took Basil's hand and squeezed it. He had never met anyone who loved food more than Basil did.

"I'm really sorry about what happened before."

Basil looked at him with wide eyes. "I know, it was a tense moment, you didn't mean anything by it."

"Well, yes, but it's lunch time and you said you weren't hungry."

"It's this business with the car." Basil looked moodily out over the flat surface of Lake Taupo as they approached it. "What will we do if they can't fix it in time? The hotel in Napier is expecting us before six."

Sebastian shrugged. "We can find a place to stay here, and call the hotel and let them know we'll be there tomorrow."

"But it's probably too late to get a refund on the room for tonight." Basil's face was a picture of tragedy.

"That's okay." Sebastian stopped walking and took both of Basil's hands, pulling him around to face him. "It's really all right. Whatever happens, it will be fine. Hotels have people cancel all the time, and I can afford to cover an extra night in Taupo if you're worried about the money."

Basil frowned and looked deep into Sebastian's eyes, searching for something. "It's not the money, well it is, but it's such a waste." He huffed and looked out over the lake again.

"How about you talk through what's really bothering you and then we can work it out together." Sebastian looked around and saw his favourite cafè. "Over some coffee and cake? This place has amazing desserts."

"All right." Basil followed meekly as Sebastian tugged him

towards the restaurant. It was open all day and into the night and Sebastian often stopped to eat there.

"You'll like this place. They do fresh scones every morning with homemade jam, and at night they do pizzas in a wood-fired oven. Their steak is really good, and you can even get little bundles of shortbread or cookies to take home."

Basil's response was a bit more interested. "I do like shortbread."

Sebastian got them a table out the front, so they could enjoy the fresh air and the view of the lake. They also had a view of the rotating dessert cabinet, which immediately caught Basil's eye.

He licked his lips.

"Perhaps I am a bit hungry after all."

Sebastian passed him the menu, which was a beast, covering everything from breakfast to cocktails. He skimmed it to see what had changed since he was last there. His shoulders were a still tense. He didn't like seeing Basil distressed. Why would a bit of disruption be such a cause for angst? it was a hiccup, perhaps a chance for a bit of extra adventure.

Maybe he needed to help Basil to see it that way?

"I think I'll get cottage pie. This place does Foxton Fizz, we have to get that," he said.

"Foxton Fizz?" Basil blinked at Sebastian. "Am I supposed to know what that is?"

"It's soda, they make it in Foxton."

"Which is…?"

"Further South, on the way to Wellington. You've really never heard of it?"

"No, I haven't travelled much outside of Auckland, remember?"

"Well, growing up in Wellington we had to drive though Foxton pretty often, it's close to Bulls. Anyway they have their own soda and it's pretty nice. Not many places still do creaming soda, and that's my favourite." Sebastian smiled up at the waiter as he approached.

"Are you ready to order?" The waiter set a pitcher of water on the table and two glasses.

"Basil?" Sebastian said. "I am if you are."

"Yes. I'll take the warm garlic bread to start and the lamb shank, both sound utterly delightful, thank you."

Sebastian raised his eyebrows. For someone who had very recently said he wasn't hungry, that was a good amount of food. Sebastian ordered his cottage pie and a bottle of Foxton Fizz creaming soda.

"Make that two," Basil said. "I'd never heard of it before now and I simply must try it for myself."

"It's worth it." The waiter read back their order and then left them to it.

"You've perked up." Sebastian couldn't keep the fondness out of his voice, so he reached for Basil's hand.

"I suppose. The food does look very good."

It was chilly under the shade, and Basil's hand felt cold. "I think there's blankets you can use if you're cold." He looked around and spotted a basket of red fleece blankets. He retrieved one for Basil, who smiled as he tucked it around his legs.

"Are you all right, though? Really?" Sebastian sat down and again took Basil's hands.

"Yes, I'm just…" Basil sighed. "We had a plan, you know? And what if there's no rooms available tonight, and we have nowhere to sleep?"

"Taupo is a tourist trap, there will be lots of places to stay. I have a travel app on my phone, I can find a good deal."

"Somewhere with a bath?"

"If that's what you want, then yeah. But hey, maybe we won't need it? The mechanics haven't called yet."

CHAPTER ELEVEN

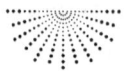

*L*unch was delicious, as Sebastian had promised. The warm, hearty food did a lot of work soothing Basil's frayed nerves. He had almost forgotten that this wasn't a scheduled stop. He was mopping up gravy with a bit of garlic bread when Sebastian's phone rang and Basil remembered. The mechanics. It felt as if fate was about to tip the scales one way or another.

"This is Sebastian." There was a pause, Basil couldn't make out the other side of the conversation, but Sebastian nodded and made solemn affirmative noises to show he was listening. "Okay, we'll come grab our bags and things then. Yeah in the next half hour, we're finishing lunch. Yup, see you soon."

He put his phone down. "They'll get delivery of the part they need first thing tomorrow and we'll be good to go midmorning."

Basil sighed. "Yes, I deduced that we'd be staying when you said we'd get our bags."

Sebastian picked up his phone again. "Give me five minutes and I'll find us a nice place to stay tonight."

Basil downed the last of his Foxton Fizz. It was very sweet, but he liked it. Perhaps he needed the sugar. His stomach was clenching with worry again but he tried to release it. Sebastian was booking them a room right this second. Sebastian would look after him. If they had to call the hotel in Napier and cancel tonight, so be it, worse things had happened. Objectively, they'd be fine.

So why did he feel like the world was falling apart?

He had to pull himself together. Act like nothing was bothering him. Sebastian wasn't bothered, after all, it came so easy to him. Be like Sebastian, nothing much ever bothered him. Well. He'd been quite tense driving the car as it failed, but that would bother anyone. Sebastian had such a good, easy-going way about him. Could Basil ever pull off an attitude like that?

"Here." Sebastian showed Basil his phone, showing a picture of a pleasantly modern hotel suite, done in whites and greys. "How about this place? It's right up the road, four stars, and has a heated swimming pool as well as a bath in the room."

Basil's stomach knot loosened. "That does look lovely."

"Great, I get a discount because I use this app so often. Well, I used to." Sebastian tapped the phone screen a few times and beamed up at Basil. "All booked. We have a couple of hours until check in, so what would you like to do? We could get dessert here, or go for a wander of the shops, or up the beach?"

Basil rubbed his stomach. "I'm full, but perhaps we could come back here for dinner and I could get dessert then?"

"That's easily done."

"In that case, a walk would be just the thing."

They went for a long, rambling walk up the lakeside path. The slight wind had a chill to it. Basil wished he'd thought to grab a scarf from the car, but he couldn't deny the vista was stunning. The lake stretched out, almost entirely still, towards the mountains on the South side.

They paused on a little wooden platform to look across to the mountains, and Basil slipped his arm through Sebastian's and leaned against him.

"Which mountain is which?"

"The big sprawly one is Ruapehu. The pointy cone one is Tongariro," Sebastian pointed with his free hand. "The Legend is that Ruapehu was married to Taranaki, but then she fell in love with Tongariro. Taranaki got so angry that he stormed off to the East coast, but he can still see them both." He sketched a line towards the West. "Ruapehu missed him and that's why she still steams or smokes sometimes, and Tongariro smokes because he's angry he doesn't have her undivided attention."

Basil chuckled. "Poor old Taranaki."

"Yeah." Sebastian slipped his arms around Basil's waist and cuddled him from behind. Basil felt the knot in his stomach loosen more. "But I always loved the idea of jealous volcanos. I first read that story as a kid at the National Park info centre. Fun, isn't it?"

"It is."

"They say the Whanganui river is the path he carved out as he stormed off. I looked on a map and it's a bit meandering but it does connect up."

"That's lovely." Basil relaxed back into Sebastian's arms. "I like listening to you tell stories. I think that's why your show is so popular, you have a knack for storytelling."

"Ahh… thank you." Sebastian sounded embarrassed, so Basil didn't push it further.

"How about we head back past some shops?" Basil said. "Since we have the time, we may as well see what Taupo has to offer."

"Great idea."

By the time they got to the hotel room, Basil had a few bags of souvenirs and even a couple of second-hand books from op shops. Sebastian had called the Napier hotel as Basil perused the shelves, and that had laid a few more of Basil's worries to rest.

The room was absolutely stunning, even nicer than the photos. Basil collapsed onto the bed with a sigh, his fingers rubbing the creamy cotton sheets between his fingers.

The last of his worries ebbed as he thought about what a good night's sleep he was going to have.

Sebastian set down their suitcases then flopped down beside him. "This is a pretty good outcome, don't you think?"

"It is." Basil leaned over to give him a kiss. "I'm sorry for freaking out. I had my schedule and everything and I felt…"

"I know."

That night they did indeed return to the same cafe for dinner, sitting inside in one of the high backed booths for warmth as the temperature had dropped several degrees when the sun went down.

This time Basil ordered the barbeque ribs and Sebastian had a fillet of salmon with a teriyaki glaze. Although it had been delicious, Basil didn't order the garlic bread again. He wanted to save space for one of the alluring -looking desserts.

They were half-way through eating dinner when a vaguely familiar voice said "Hello again."

Basil looked up to see the man who'd been staying at the Waitomo Caves Hotel with them. He wore a sleek black sweater and suede jacket with his dress pants. He smirked down at them, his skin sallow compared to the black of his clothes.

"Oh, Asher, wasn't it? How about that, you're here too?" Sebastian set his knife and fork down and went to shake Asher's hand.

Basil fought the wild urge to slap Sebastian's hand away like he was reaching for a burning hot fire

He resisted, but only barely.

Asher and Sebastian shook hands.

"Yes, I'm dropping through on my tour of the North Island." Asher let go of Sebastian's hand and turned to Basil. "I hope you're quite recovered from your little turn in the cave. Gave us all a fright didn't you?"

There was something hungry in his eyes that Basil didn't like one bit. His magic stirred inside him, as if ready to defend him from an attack. But Asher wasn't attacking, he was making polite conversation.

Basil struggled to find words to respond to Asher's question. "Fine, yes, I'm fine."

"I'm so pleased to hear it."

Asher's smile got wider. He seemed to have too many teeth. Basil's skin crawled. He wanted to grab Sebastian and run as far as possible from this man immediately, dessert be damned!

But again, nothing Asher had said was out of line. Why then did his ever fibre scream of possible danger?

"Well, I shall leave you two fine gentlemen to your meal. Have a lovely evening." Asher wiggled his fingers and turned, walking straight out the door.

"Odd to have run into him again." Sebastian speared a forkful of salmon and offered it to Basil. "Try this."

Basil took the mouthful and hummed appreciation as he chewed it. "That's divine." He glanced behind him to be sure that Asher was really gone before leaning over his plate to talk to Sebastian in a hushed tone. "I don't like that man. In fact, I feel like he's hiding something, or planning something."

A small crinkle formed between Sebastian's eyebrows. "Really? He seems normal to me."

That surprised Basil. Sebastian was more likely to think the best of people, but he was also pretty savvy about who was worth trusting. Perhaps that handshake had been more than a handshake?

He had sudden terrible visions of Asher using the skin-to-skin touch to make Sebastian trust him, or possibly lay a spell over him.

Basil checked his pocket for a crystal that wasn't there. He'd left them all in his bag in the hotel room. Well, he could give Sebastian a magical scan and ensure there was nothing magical affecting him after dinner.

Or perhaps Basil was letting his anxiety from earlier in the day make him paranoid.

Sebastian was watching him. He probably expected a response. Basil cleared his throat.

"I get a bad feeling, but more than that, just now my magic stirred. Right as he was standing there. It only does that if I feel I'm in danger. Maybe it's nothing, maybe I'm overreacting, but I don't like him."

Sebastian nodded slowly. "Well, chances are we won't see him again."

"I hope not."

They finished up their meals, and ordered a dessert each. Basil's mood lightened at the taste of his slice of chocolate cake.

Surely he had been overreacting, making something out of nothing. He had been so anxious before, his adrenaline was probably still up and making his brain panic.

They paid and left the restaurant to walk arm in arm back towards the hotel. At nighttime the lights illuminated only the shore part of the lake, the rest vanished into darkness. Basil looked out into the void and was comforted to know there were mountains out there.

"Oh look, a second hand shop we missed." Sebastian's words tore Basil's attention from the darkness to look around.

"Really?"

Sebastian led him to the door of a quaint-looking little shop. The window had old-fashioned lettering proclaiming 'Oddments and Curiosities.'

Basil could see a floor to ceiling shelf of books. The opening hours indicated they only opened in the evenings. "Let's go in and have a look."

Sebastian opened the door to the shop and held it for Basil. He felt a frisson of magic as he walked in and looked around for the shopkeeper.

In back an old woman stooped behind the counter. She raised a gnarled hand in greeting. "Evening dearies, have a look around."

"Thank you," Sebastian said.

Basil smiled and waved back, recognising a fellow witch when he saw one. "Thank you, lovely collection of books you have here." The woman turned back to a small screen TV she was watching.

"Any questions, just ask."

CHAPTER TWELVE

*S*ebastian left Basil by the books and wandered deeper into the store. An old, worn leather camera case that drew his eye, and he went to pick it up.

The handwritten label read '*Polaroid 1970s, working cond. $20*'. A steal. Sebastian looked inside the case for the model number, and looked online to see how easy it would be to get film for it. Not too hard, a few people were selling old boxes of film on Trade Me.

He nodded to himself, turned to continue browsing. With no one else in the store he wasn't worried about someone else picking up the camera.

There was a rack of clothes, which he flicked through. Sometimes cool vintage pieces popped up in places like these. He inhaled as his fingers found a long sleeve button shirt in blue, with a pattern of frolicking golden cats amongst blooming flowers. He couldn't guess the age of it, but the cotton was woven soft as silk and when he looked into the collar to see the size it looked as if it might fit him.

He took the hanger off the rack and held it in front of him.

"Basil, what do you think?"

Basil looked over. He had three books in his right arm and he was plucking another from the shelf. "Very nice. It suits you."

Sebastian slung the shirt over his arm and kept looking. There were various knick-knacks, board games, card decks including some tarot decks. He hesitated for a moment, looking them over but none of the deck designs really spoke to him. He weighed the vintage polaroid camera in one hand and went over to Basil. "I'm getting these. What have you got?"

By now Basil had six books in his arms. "A nice edition of a Jeeves and Wooster collection, a novel I've been meaning to read by that Kiwi author who lives in Wellington, some books for identifying New Zealand plants from the fifties and this one, which is always on reserve at the library so I thought I'd give it a go."

Sebastian blinked at the title of the book Basil had shown him at the end. "Into the Mist by Lee Murray?"

"Yes, another New Zealand author. Looks fun."

"I suppose it does. Now, let's go pay before you pick up another armful of books."

Basil flushed. "Fine, be all reasonable."

The woman behind the counter stood up to serve them, and after some fussing with the EFTPOS machine, bagged up their items and wished them a good night.

They walked out into the night and back up to the hotel.

"She was a witch," Basil said.

Sebastian made a surprised noise, although it made sense when he thought about it. "Seems like the kind of place a witch would run. Especially since they only seemed to open at night."

Basil hummed his agreement. "I can't wait to look through the plant books. Perhaps I'll be able to identify the trees as we drive to Napier tomorrow."

The hotel room was pleasantly warm after the chill of the night air.

Basil ran bath, and Sebastian relaxed in front of the TV. He flicked between the channels for a while. He paused on the nightly news, there was a piece about the missing teenagers. Each of their school photos flashed on the screen.

"Police are asking anyone who might have seen them in the last three days to call in," the news anchor said.

Sebastian watched one of the teen's father's make a plea to the camera before the story changed to the next piece of news.

He channel-surfed a while longer before settling on a British murder mystery he'd seen before.

As Basil hopped into the bath, Sebastian found his eye drawn to the purple paper bag from the second-hand store. He pulled out his new shirt. He shrugged off the layers he was wearing and stood up to try it on. What luck it had been to find it in his size…? And such an interesting design. It would look great on camera, especially if he was in natural light.

His mind buzzed, imagining himself in front of a forest or standing overlooking some vista from the top of a hill, beautiful shots made even nicer by the shirt.

The sleeves hugged his biceps without being too tight, and as he buttoned it up he marvelled at how perfect the fit was.

As he fastened the last button, he felt a blast, like a static shock but much worse. His vision went black.

After a moment, he blinked his eyes open harsh light. Something terrible had happened to the room.

The couch was enormous, the carpet pile was thick and deep, and the TV was bigger than a movie screen. He swallowed, tried to call out to Basil, but all that came out of his mouth was a strangled sounding yowl.

His hands dug deeper into the carpet.

Wait, why am I on my hands and knees? Looking down he saw the truth. He didn't have hands. He had round, black furred paws.

Another yowl, this time rather terrified.

I'm a cat? Oh god, I'm a cat! What should I do?

Fear bubbled inside him and threatened to overwhelm him. He felt his back arching and his fur spiking along this spine. He eyed the closed window, with half a mind to tear out of it, escape this room, and his predicament with it. But his logical mind overwhelmed that urge. They weren't on the ground floor. The window was sealed shut. It wasn't the way to solve this problem.

Basil. He had to get to Basil.

Basil would fix this.

With only that thought in mind, he bolted towards the bathroom door. Thankfully, Basil had left it ajar.

Unfortunately running on four legs didn't come naturally to Sebastian and his lolloping gait soon tangled his legs up and he rolled head over paws into the wall.

For a moment he lay there, tangled in his own too-long limbs and unpredictable tail (tail!) and stared at the ceiling, panting. He wanted to cry.

A plaintive mew emitted from him before he clamped his jaw shut. He sounded pathetic.

He closed his eyes and took a deep breath before slowly picking himself up again. He moved slower, one paw at a time, and that way he made it through the door to the bathroom. He meowed as loudly as he could.

Basil peered over the bathtub's side. "A cat! Bastian, look! This hotel has a cute little cat!"

Sebastian-the-cat meowed again. He *was* Sebastian!

Basil reached towards him. The huge hand moving towards Sebastian's face frightened him all over again. He hissed, backing up until he hit the bathroom wall, which startled him again. He sprang back and yowled his despair.

Basil chuckled. "Bastian, you have to come and see this!"

Sebastian flopped down onto the bathmat. This was hopeless.

Basil's tone got concerned. "Bastian? Are you there?"

Sebastian mewed once.

Basil got out of the bath and hurriedly wrapped a towel

around himself. Sebastian retreated to the corner of the bathroom. Basil seemed terribly large, like Godzilla stomping around. Sebastian didn't want one of his tiny paws squished under his foot.

Basil left the room. Sebastian could hear him talking. "Sebastian's jeans and watch are here, and there's his phone, he wouldn't have gone out without those... especially the phone."

The thundering footsteps approached the bathroom again. Sebastian's ears picked up so much more than he was used to hearing. He flattened them to his head, hoping for reprieve.

When Basil appeared again, his hands glowed softly with purple light. His magic.

Thank god, he's caught on.

"Sebastian? Is that you?" Basil knelt and offered one glowing hand.

Sebastian moved forward to sniff at the hand, the way he'd seen countless cats do before. Basil smelled like safety, like a familiar bed, like family. He smelled so good Sebastian was bunting his head into his hand before he thought about it, feline instincts taking over. He mewed again, trying to convey that yes, he was Sebastian, and yes, he needed help.

"Okay, Bastian." Without warning Basil scooped Sebastian into his arms and carried him to the next room.

Being suddenly up so high was dizzying, but Basil's grip was secure, Sebastian knew he'd never drop him. His eyes took in so much detail, he could see everything with great precision and that just made it all the more startling.

The enormity of his predicament engulfed Sebastian. He made a tiny, sad mew without even meaning to.

He'd never heard of anyone being completely transformed into a cat. Therefore he'd never heard of anyone getting better from it either.

"There, there." Basil rubbed between his ears. "It's very strange, I know, but you're going to be alright."

Basil set Sebastian-the-cat down on the hotel bed, and Sebastian cried again. He didn't want to be without Basil's body heat.

"It's all right, kitty, I'm right here."

Basil had never used that pet name on him before.

Sebastian had closed his eyes in anguish, but he opened them now.

Basil was simultaneously pulling on his pyjama pants and feeling through his bag of books with his other hand. He slowly toppled over onto the carpet. "Whoops! I'm all right!"

Sebastian's hackles rose (he had hackles now!) and claws popped out of his paws with shock. He crept to the edge of the bed to peer down at his hapless witch of a boyfriend.

Basil was sitting up, pants on, flipping through the linen-bound book he used as a Book of Shadows.

Sebastian huffed a sigh, pleased that it sounded exactly as hopeless as he felt. He hadn't been aware cats could sigh. It felt satisfying.

How long am I going to be stuck in this body?

I don't want to be a cat.

I can't drive. I love driving. Basil will have to take over the driving and he doesn't love it the way he does, he never got the hang of how my car handles.

Sebastian's claws retracted and he backed up from the edge of the bed, barely aware that he was doing it.

Is this hotel even pet friendly? Are we going to get in trouble?

Am I a pet now?

How will I use the toilet? I'm too small, my paws will slide on the toilet seat, I'll fall into the water. I'll have to get Basil to hold me in place, how humiliating.

Mewing sadly, he curled into a tight ball and shut his eyes. The extra limb of his tail wrapped around him, covering his eyes. His heart, usually a slow, steady beat, now raced fast enough it might have killed him if he'd been human.

A warm hand stroked down his back.

It was the most soothing, delightful sensation. So good, his body relaxed, and that in turn soothed his mind. His instincts overwhelmed his rational brain. He stretched out of the ball and rolled on his back.

Basil's large, warm hand made him feel safe for the first time since he'd transformed. A strange vibration started in his throat. He was purring, a totally natural reaction to being petted by his loved one.

"There, that's better." Basil climbed onto the bed beside Sebastian and settled against the pillows. Sebastian rolled onto his front so he could climb into Basil's lap and read the book as he did.

There was something comforting about being so small, about fitting so easily into Basil's lap as he read, as his hand absent-mindedly pet his fur.

Basil flipped pages slowly, looking for something that would help.

Despite all his fears and terrors, Sebastian started to doze, the rumble in his throat soothing him to a dreamless sleep.

CHAPTER THIRTEEN

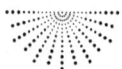

*B*asil felt remarkably free of panic. It was pleasant to know that when something absolutely catastrophic happened to his boyfriend, no pun intended, he could keep a level head and think about solutions.

Feeling a whisper of magic in his fingertips, he flicked the pages faster.

He wasn't exactly sure what he might find in his book of shadows. He had carefully handwritten every page, but at the same time, the book was capable of surprising him. His mother had described the nature of such books as a sort of doublethink experiment.

The book was absolutely devoted to Basil, and it was his personal book of magic. But it was also connected to some universal *other* that could tap into the knowledge of all witches in some peculiar and ancient magic. Basil had vowed to study it someday. After all, books were his speciality. He'd never quite found the time. Besides, where did you start with something like that?

Focus on the problem at hand, Basil.

He cleared his throat and glanced down at Sebastian. A warm, furry stretched out picture of kitty contentment, draped over his lap. He felt a swell of affection but set it aside. He wanted a cat, sure, but he wanted his boyfriend more. Sebastian had displayed a lot of fear and sadness. The sooner Basil could resolve the cause of it, the better.

He flipped a page of his book and found something promising. "A restoration of usual form," he read aloud. He didn't remember writing these words, and the handwriting didn't look familiar. That was all right. This was what he needed.

Requirements: the place the curse or unwanted change had taken place

A curse… who would have cursed him? Surely not that nice little lady in the shop. Or possibly it was, maybe she existed simply to sow chaos. People like that did exist, although Basil had never encountered one before.

Poor Bastian.

Well, at least he knew where the change had taken place. It was right here in this room right where Sebastian's jeans were still crumpled on the floor.

What else?

"Candles, ginger for any pain, a butterfly's wing for transformation…." He trailed off. He could track down ginger, they had that at the supermarket, but a butterfly's wing?

He picked up his phone and called his mother.

Dawn answered after three rings.

"Basil, sweetie, how are you? How's the holiday? You're not calling to get me to come and pick you up are you? I had a few wines already."

"Mum, I'm not a teenager anymore." Basil rolled his eyes. "I'm calling about something serious."

"Well, you always made those sleepovers you weren't enjoying sound very serious, darling."

Basil rubbed Sebastian between the ears, encouraging him to stay asleep. "Mum. Please, just listen? Actually, is Dad there too? You could put me on speaker, I might want his advice as well."

"Yeah, he's here, hold on. How do I do speakerphone?"

There was a rustling sound, and Basil could hear his father's voice giving advice.

After a moment, there was a change in the quality of the call. Basil cleared his throat. "Can you hear me?"

"Yes, we can hear you." Russ sounded a little miffed. Probably Dawn had ignored him.

"Good. Right. Well, the problem is that Sebastian's been turned into a cat."

There was a pause.

Basil bit his lip. Had he made a terrible mistake in calling his parents?

"A cat?" Russ said faintly.

He hurriedly added more information. "I don't know, it just happened really suddenly. I found something in my Book of Shadows but it says I need a butterfly's wing and I'm pretty sure all the shops in Taupo have closed by now."

"Aw, you're in Taupo? It's so lovely this time of year." Dawn sounded envious. "Get a photo of the lake for me, will you?"

"Mum, please focus will you? My boyfriend is a cat!"

Basil had raised his voice loud enough that Sebastian sat up, blinking sleepily at him.

"What kind of cat?" That was Russ.

"Um, black cat, domestic shorthair. Does it make a difference?"

"I don't think so, I'm curious." There was a rustling sound. "Butterfly wings will be there because of the metamorphosis that the caterpillar undergoes. I'm pretty sure there's a plant you can use to replace it, give me a minute while I look it up."

"If you have enough will and summon enough magic, say with a good circle and some crystals, a picture of a butterfly will work just as well, love." That was Dawn, getting serious finally.

"Really?" Basil breathed out. "I brought crystals and salts and things so I can probably do that."

"Oh, well, that's true. Here, it's lupins. Do you have any lupins with you?"

"Strangely enough, no, I didn't travel with lupins, Dad." Sebastian bumped his head against Basil's chin. "Hey, are you okay?"

Sebastian mewed pitifully and tapped his paw on Basil's leg, then looked significantly at the glass of water Basil had beside the bed. He picked it up and offered it to Sebastian.

"Was that him? He sounds adorable!" Dawn exclaimed.

Sebastian shook his head and made a sort of grumbling noise that Basil hadn't known cats were capable of. He tipped the glass. Sebastian leaned in to lick at the surface of the water.

"Right, so if I make a strong enough circle, and use some crystals to channel my power, I should be able to substitute the elements?"

"That's right. Magic is about intent more than anything else, you know that."

"Right, Mum, yeah I remember you saying something along those lines when I was a kid."

Sebastian pulled back from the glass and delicately wiped his whiskers with his paw.

"Mum, Dad, have you ever heard of something like this happening before?"

"Yes, your aunt Agatha," Russ said. "Tripped a curse left by some kids playing silly buggers and turned into a Norfolk terrier. Took us two days to chase her down, she was having so much fun."

Basil felt a knot loosen in his stomach. "But you reversed it."

"Of course."

"She didn't want us to, which slowed the process somewhat," Russ added.

"I don't think I have that problem. Sebastian seems keen to turn back."

Sebastian looked up from licking water and gave a deliberate kitty nod.

"Should be a doddle then. Set up your circle, envision the elements you need and pour your will into it. Sebastian can add his desire to change back as well." There was the sound of Dawn smacking her lips. "But send some pictures of him as a cat first, I'm sure he's adorable."

Sebastian grumbled again.

Basil set down the glass so he could gently rub his fluffy cheek. "He's the cutest cat I've ever seen."

"Remember that the spell, once you've done it, might not work instantly," Russ said. "You might need to give it overnight to properly set. Transformations can be tricky that way."

"Right, good to know. Thanks Dad, thanks Mum. I'll, uh, send you some pictures."

Sebastian flopped dramatically over Basil's lap as he hung up the phone.

Basil rubbed his ears. "That was excellent news. Come on, let's get this spell sorted and then we can go to bed, then when we wake up, it should be all over. That sounds good, doesn't it? I'll just whip to the loo quickly."

Basil used the bathroom and found himself staring at himself in the mirror as he washed his hands. He looked overwhelmed. He'd put on a brave face for Sebastian, but he wasn't actually sure at all he was capable of such a spell. He'd never done anything like it before.

How had this even happened? Was it the shirt Sebastian had bought at the op shop? That little old lady? No. Before then. Basil remembered Sebastian shaking Asher's hand, and his own visceral reaction to it. *I'd wanted to stop them, to protect Bastian. I must have felt something, on some level. But could a transformation spell be so simple to cast? I hadn't felt any magic coming from Asher, and they only shook hands for a moment.*

Stars, am I being paranoid?

Is it possible to overreact to your boyfriend being changed into a cat? Or is this the correct amount of panic?

He took a deep breath and stared himself down in the mirror. "You've got this, Basil. You've done all sorts of magic you didn't know you were capable of. And Sebastian is relying on you." He gave himself this pep talk *sotto voce* so as not to alarm Sebastian.

He pulled on his pyjama top and walked back out. "Right, let's get this started."

Sebastian mewed and pulled himself to standing with visible effort. He stretched, arching his back and lowering his front half while he yawned. Basil cooed and snapped some photos which he immediately sent to his mother.

"Right, focus. A circle, lucky I brought some candles with me, just in case…"

Sebastian hopped to the floor and trotted to his camera gear bag. He patted it with one paw and meowed louder than Basil had heard him previously.

"What? You… you want me to film this, are you sure?"

Again the kitty nodded with precision.

"Stars, of course you do."

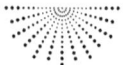

CHAPTER FOURTEEN

*I*t was a special kind of torture, watching Basil set up the camera. He'd seen Sebastian do it enough times that he knew the basic idea, but he didn't have the practice. Sebastian winced as Basil almost dropped the camera lens, but it was caught with sparkling purple magic.

"Okay, I attach this to the tripod here… and then I have to… blast it!" More magic mist appeared, and the tripod extended itself. Basil screwed the camera into place.

He bent to look through it.

`Sebastian mewed to alert him to the lens cap. Stretching up to tap it with his paw.

Basil reached around and removed it. "Right you are. Now, if I press the autofocus that should… yes, that seems to have worked. I'm going to start it recording and you can edit and do your voice over and all that later, yes? One meow for yes, two for no."

Sebastian sighed and meowed once. He hoped very much that they wouldn't need that code for much longer.

Basil moved from behind the camera and moved around the space in front of it, setting candles in little brass holders onto the carpet. Sebastian knew he'd brought a few witchy things with him but he'd had no idea that it included little brass candle holders. Still, he couldn't complain about that now that they were being used for his benefit.

A cat instinct overtook him and he pressed his side against Basil's legs, winding through them and feeling his body flood with affection. Being a cat wasn't entirely horrible.

He didn't want to stay one, that was for sure, but it wasn't all bad. His emotions became everything he was. Which was unpleasant when the emotion was terror, but very nice indeed when he was feeling love.

Sebastian's sensitive nose twitched as Basil lit the candles. He used his magic to do it, casting a flame on his finger and touching it to each of the wicks, before pointing up at the room's smoke detector and shushing it, although it hadn't made any noise. He turned back to Sebastian.

"You sit here, in the middle, and I'll sit facing the camera, yes?"

That seemed like a good set up so Sebastian mewed once and then settled in the centre, in front of Basil and facing the camera. He wondered how this shot would look. How strange it would be to see a small cat on the footage and know it was him. How would his audience take all of this? It was so bizarre, but then, that's what his channel was about.

Basil stroked his back with a gentle hand. "It's all right, Bastian. I'm fixing this now."

Sebastian felt the rumble of a purr again and closed his eyes, enjoying the sensation, and the soothing power of Basil's hand.

Sebastian's ears picked up the clack of crystals, and then the magic started. Sebastian could feel it, which was new and different. He usually couldn't feel anything at all when Basil did magic, but perhaps cats had an extra sense?

It felt like danger, first and foremost. Sebastian's hackles rose. He breathed quickly through his nose and tried to focus on trust. He trusted Basil and he very much wanted to be a human again.

The urge rose again to flee and he had to

Basil's magic felt like a storm brewing. Pressure in the air and nascent danger. Sebastian curled his tail tight around his legs and steadfastly weathered the change in atmosphere.

Behind him, Basil started to speak, words that had magic woven into them, that crackled in Sebastian's ears and made him wince.

He blinked as the fluttering wings of a butterfly appeared beside him. Beautiful and purple, but faint. Sebastian could see the carpet through it. A magical illusion? It was very good. His cat instincts wanted to pounce on it. He gave in and swatted a paw at the butterfly as it came closer. It would make good footage he reasoned, and more than that it would stop him concentrating on how the magic felt.

Behind him he heard Basil chuckle as he wove some more magic. Some illusory bundles of herbs appeared on the ground.

Then Basil's words changed, and he felt his hand on his back. Sebastian's ears filled with a roaring sound, static and thunder rolled into one. He cringed, ears flattening, trying to escape, but knowing he shouldn't. Basil's hands lifted him into his lap and patted him firmly, holding him in place as the magic seeped into Sebastian's skin. He felt every inch of fur as it lifted, just enough to let the magic underneath, before settling back into place. He wanted to scream, to run, to escape by any means necessary. If Basil hadn't been holding him he might have bolted into the night never to be changed back. It didn't hurt, exactly, but the sensation was so unnatural, so disturbing that it had the same effect.

He was probably yowling. He couldn't tell, the roaring filled his ears still and he didn't dare open his eyes. He didn't want to see his paws distort, or any kind of magic on him.

After what felt like an eternity, the feeling faded, and the sound died away. He blinked his eyes open fearfully, to find he was sprawled over Basil's lap, all four legs extended as long as they'd go. He was panting heavily, and although the instinct to run was still there, he felt far too exhausted to move.

"That seems to be the last of it," Basil's voice sounded rough. He picked up a clear crystal and rolled it slowly down Sebastian's spine.

"How are you feeling, Bastian? Okay?"

One meow for yes. But I don't feel okay, not really. I feel like I've been through the washing machine. But if I say no Basil might do more magic and I don't want that either.

"Meow."

"Good kitty." Basil stroked him gently. He tipped his face up to address the camera. "I think we're about done. The spell is on him now, and it requires sleep and time to activate. I'm going to shut off the camera and with any luck the next face you see will be Sebastian's human one."

Sebastian felt himself lifted into the air. Basil moved around the room, turning off the camera, extinguishing candles, turning off lights.

He pulled the blankets on the bed back and set Sebastian down on the sheet before sliding in behind him.

"You did really well, Bastian. My brave little kitty. I'm sorry if it hurts, I'm so sorry. But I think the spell went all right, and you should be better after a sleep. Back to normal. I see the magic settling into you, and it's moving slowly but it's there."

Sebastian didn't have any energy to respond. He stretched himself out as Basil pulled the blankets over them and pressed against Basil's warm chest. Despite his exhaustion and feeling wrung out from the ordeal of the spell, a purr started up in his throat as Basil softly stroked his fur.

Sebastian woke to the sound of his phone ringing. He blinked his eyes open and reached for it. He'd been in the deepest sleep he could remember ever having, dreamless and velvet-black. He picked up the phone. The mechanic was calling. He tapped the answer button.

"This is Bastian…" he said, voice rumbly with sleep. No. He was purring. No, he was… He looked at his hand. A hand. He was a human again. He fell back on the pillow with a relieved sigh.

"Hey, yeah this is Gavin your car is all sorted." Gavin said in one breath, almost in one word. "Ready for pick up."

"That's fantastic, thank you. We'll get some breakfast and then come get it. Thank you."

Sebastian hung up and turned towards Basil. Somehow, he'd slept through the whole conversation. Maybe the spell had worn him out too?

Sebastian leaned in to touch him ever so gently on the nose. "Meow?"

Basil's face screwed up, trying to get away from the tickle and then his eyes flew open. "Oh no, it didn't work! It…" His panic died off as he looked into Sebastian's face. His expression broke into relief and affectionate annoyance. "It did work. Did you just meow at me?"

"I might have." Sebastian pulled Basil into his arms and squeezed him tight. "Thank you, for everything, for keeping your head while I freaked out, and for doing the spell."

Basil hummed, snuggling in close to Sebastian. "Well, of course. What's a boyfriend for if not reversing a transformation spell?"

"We should get that on a mug."

Basil chuckled, his hand gently stroking Sebastian's back as if he were still a cat. "I'm so sorry that it seemed like an ordeal for you. You were all hissing and backing away and yowling." Being petted was remarkably soothing, Sebastian hoped this was a new habit.

.   .   .

90

"It was frightening. I could sense your magic, which isn't something I've ever felt before, and it felt like a threat. Like danger. But I'd far rather have gone through that to become a man again than the alternative."

"Indeed." Basil kissed him softly. "It's good to have you back, kitty."

Now it was Sebastian's turn to scrunch up his face, but in truth he liked the pet name.

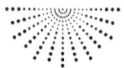

CHAPTER FIFTEEN

*B*asil looked out the window as Lake Taupo disappeared behind them and they wound their way up the hill into pine forests. He wasn't sad to leave Taupo behind. It had been much more stressful than anticipated, but at the same time he wished they'd done more sightseeing.

"It should be a two hour drive, unless we come across some roadworks," Sebastian said.

Basil turned his attention to his beautiful, human boyfriend and felt his tension ease. He loved him so much, and he was overjoyed that he wasn't a cat anymore.

The shirt Sebastian had put on had still been on him when he turned back into a human. Basil had looked over every stitch in it with his second sight and found nothing untoward. Which didn't necessarily mean it was an innocent item, Basil's reversal spell could have removed all evidence.

They'd had fresh scones at the same restaurant they'd eaten at the day before, picked up the car, and driven straight out of town. Sebastian took the way that meant they drove past the second-hand store from the night before. It was closed tight, and in fact, looked like it had been closed for some time. There was nothing on display in the window, and the painted sign was chipped and faded.

Peculiar.

Sebastian hadn't said anything, but continued to drive out of town. Basil hadn't pushed him.

As the morning wore on, the pine forests gave way to farmland, lush and green from winter rains, and lots of little hills and dips. Often they'd turn a corner, or crest a hill to find a brand new view. It was delightful.

Sebastian was uncharacteristically quiet as he drove. He'd put on a particularly chill playlist, which suited the prettiness of the countryside. Basil was worried that Sebastian was brooding when he made an 'Mm!' noise, indicated and pulled over to the side of the road.

There, in the wide mouth of a gravel driveway was a wooden cart with a hand painted sign *'new season kiwifruit, oranges'*

"I've stopped here before," Sebastian said. "Their fruit is always the absolute best."

"Jolly good." Basil got out of the car to follow Sebastian, pleased that something had made him smile, even if the sudden unplanned stop jangled on his nerves just a touch. It was worth it.

Sebastian made a selection from the bagged fruits on display and left a twenty dollar bill in the honesty box. Two bags of oranges and two of kiwifruit. When Basil did the maths it came to far less than that, but Sebastian didn't seem at all concerned about change. As they headed back to the car, Sebastian handed the fruit to Basil.

"I guess it's not particularly easy to eat these in the car, but the smell of the oranges alone…"

Basil lifted a paper bag of oranges to his face and inhaled. It was perfect, the zesty scent of ripe oranges. So fresh.

"I'd never have thought to stop at a place like this. These smell amazing."

A car zoomed around the corner. Sebastian startled, moving closer to Basil before visibly relaxing when he saw it was a car.

"It's all right." Basil stowed the fruit in the back seat of the car and then put his arms around Sebastian. "Do you want me to drive for a bit?"

Sebastian sagged against Basil and huffed out a heavy sigh. "No. I'm sorry, after last night I feel jumpy. But driving calms me down, it's a good focus."

"No need to apologise." Basil rubbed his back. "But the offer is there if you need it, all right?"

"Yeah." Sebastian kissed Basil's cheek. "You're sweet, thank you. I dunno if the cat instincts are still kinda there, or... I was a lot more everything while I was a cat. If I was happy I was totally happy, if I was startled I was terrified. It's hard to forget."

Basil hummed in sympathy. "I'm sure the memory will fade with time. I wish we could have got to the bottom of it all."

"Me too."

Sebastian looked briefly lost and miserable, so Basil hugged him tighter again. "It's going to be alright." His words sounded firm and sure of himself, but his stomach fell away as he spoke. He had no idea what had caused the curse. He had a couple of suspicions, people who he might never see again, but no idea how to protect Sebastian from something like that happening again.

Maybe he needed to do some reading on personal protection amulets. That would probably be a smart idea.

They kissed, Basil trying to pour his desire to protect Sebastian into the kiss.

Sebastian pulled away quickly. "Come on, let's get to Napier."

The grey skies they'd been driving under gave way at much the same time the farmland started to turn into vineyards and orchards.

The sunshine seemed to lift Sebastian's spirits as he navigated them through the small town to the waterfront promenade that their hotel was situated on.

"I booked us one of the classic Art Deco hotels," Sebastian said. "Built pretty soon after the big quake."

This was something Basil had read up about. In 1931 a huge earthquake flattened half of the city. When rebuilding, the town had embraced Art Deco, making Napier a lush Art Deco city. Once a year they even had Deco weekends. People dressed like it was the thirties, driving old-fashioned cars and listening to live jazz. Basil thought he might quite like to return for one of those weekends.

He'd made a list of the things he'd like to do while in town, including visiting the independent bookstore, the museum and the National aquarium. They'd made very good time and had a fair chunk of the afternoon still free, but he didn't want to push Sebastian. Perhaps what he needed was a restful afternoon with some good food and nothing much to do.

He brooded while they checked into the hotel. It was a grand affair, with a marble check in counter and a grand staircase with wooden railings and a boldly striped carpet. A comfortable looking sitting area was tastefully cluttered with wing-back chairs and low coffee tables. Double doors led to an old-fashioned bar and restaurant. On the check in counter stood a lamp which was made up of a tiny metal statue of a woman, all sleek lines as she held out the glowing glass orb that contained the lightbulb.

Basil felt as if he ought to be wearing a straw boater.

"You're a little early," the concierge said. "We are happy to take your bags, but your room won't be ready until three."

"That's fine." They passed their cases and bags over and strolled back out the front entrance.

Basil checked his watch. One thirty. "What would you like to do?" He slipped his arm through Sebastian's. "We could find somewhere to have lunch? Go for a walk up the waterfront? Maybe sit and have an ice-cream?"

Sebastian glanced at him. "I thought you wanted to go to the museum and things?"

Basil shrugged and tried to look like he didn't much care what they did. "Those things can wait until tomorrow."

Sebastian pulled his arm so they were standing closer together as he stopped on the footpath. "Why? We have time, we can knock them off this afternoon."

"Right, but..." Basil dithered, trying to think of an excuse. Nothing came to mind so blurted the truth. "I want to do something that soothes you. You've been all quiet and jumpy. If you want a quiet afternoon then I'm absolutely happy with that. I want to look after you a bit."

Sebastian smiled softly. "That's kind of you."

He took a breath. "How about lunch, and then we have a walk? I think Pania of the Reef is nearby and I'd like to see her."

"That sounds perfect."

They found a charming little Italian restaurant and had a hearty pasta lunch, taking their time and relaxing over a glass of white wine each. Sebastian still didn't seem inclined to talk, so Basil filled up the silence by telling him about the novel he was reading. Sebastian seemed content to listen, smiling faintly now and then.

By the time they were done with lunch and ready for their walk the temperature had dropped. The sun wasn't yet close to setting but it was heading towards the horizon.

"I can't wait for summer," Basil said. "I bet it's beautiful here in summer."

'It's beautiful now."

Marine Parade was long and straight, but on the ocean side of the road, which was entirely clear of houses and hotels, there was a gently winding pathway. They strolled together, arm in arm, past the iconic fountain, under trees and past sculptures.

Basil now didn't feel the need to fill the silence. Listening to the roar of the surf on the rocky shore, and taking in the sights, they walked in companionable quiet.

"There!" Sebastian pointed. "There she is."

They approached the bronze statue of a young woman seated looking out to sea.

"Ah, she's beautiful." Basil snapped some photos with his phone. Sebastian's expression softened, watching.

"I try and stop in and visit her every time I'm in town." Sebastian touched his fingertips to one of her shiny knees. "She feels like good luck, although her story is pretty tragic."

"I know this one," Basil said. "Let me remember... she's a creature of the sea, like a mermaid, and she fell in love with a boy on the land. They got married, but she had to go to the sea every day. He tried to trap her with..." Basil searched his memory, sorting one mermaid story from another. "He tried to feed her cooked food, which would trap her on land but she woke up and fled to the sea."

"A ruru warned her." Sebastian looked around at the city street, decorative trees and traffic. "Back before the city was built I guess it was pretty forested here, a nicer spot for owls. A ruru warned her and she went into the sea, never to return. They say she became the reef."

"It's amazing to me how often cultures have stories which are similar," Basil mused. "It's not the same story as a selkie, a crane wife, or the little mermaid, but... it's not really that different either."

"Makes you wonder what's under there, doesn't it?" Sebastian slipped his arm around Basil's shoulder and they looked out at the crashing waves of the Pacific. Signs all along the beach warned people not to swim. Beyond the breakers, there was a steep drop off. The signs mentioned rips which could quickly whip someone out to sea.

"Could be anything," Basil said. "Taniwha, merfolk,

kraken…" He looked up at Sebastian. "Oh stars, please don't tell me you want to film underwater as well. You do, don't you?"

Sebastian's smile was rueful. "I won't lie, I've definitely thought about it. But… I think I have to leave that to the experts. Oceanographers and marine biologists, it's all just too unpredictable out there, and besides. I used to have a recurring nightmare about a shark."

Basil's shoulders sagged with relief. "Good."

Sebastian laughed. "You were worried about having to follow me into the ocean, weren't you."

"Maybe a bit."

"No worries, I'm content on land."

Basil kissed his cheek. They nodded to Pania in respect and continued to walk.

Basil wanted to keep Sebastian talking, lighten him up a bit. "I know you said you got into ghost hunting at boarding school but you never told me any more than that."

Sebastian took his hand. "Well, school sucked, and I was always a curious kid. When I was little, I was always making up stories, and chasing my tail around the garden imagining fairies and things. I always wanted a sibling, so I imagined I had one, that I was telling them the stories, or getting them to play along in my made-up TV shows and plays and stuff." Sebastian chuckled, looking out to the ocean for a moment. "Sometimes one of the neighbour's kids would come around, or my mum would visit her friends with kids. I got on well with them, but they usually wanted to play video games. I liked video games okay but I wanted to be the one telling the story, making the decisions."

"I bet you did." Basil bumped his shoulder gently against Sebastian's.

"I went to the library a lot and I found this section in non-fiction, and this one book. *The Usborne Book of Ghosts.*"

"I know that one," Basil said. "My dad had to take it off me because it was giving me nightmares."

Sebastian chuckled. "It did have some pretty gnarly pictures in it. For me it was a whole new world. I read and re-read that book so many times, I could have recited it. And the fact that there were stories from all over the world... Just like with Pania and the people from the ocean, really. To me there was never any question, ghosts were real, and I wanted to make other people see that. When I got to boarding school and there was a real ghost in the attic I felt like... I dunno, everything slotted into place. This was what I was put on Earth to do. Does that make sense?"

"When I first got a library job I felt that same way."

Sebastian let go of Basil's hand so he could slip his arm around him. "You get it."

"The other one in that series that Dad took off me was the *Book of Monsters*." Basil leaned against Sebastian, putting his arm around his waist, glad of his body warmth as the wind picked up. "Did you read that one?"

"Of course! I used it to do a school project once." Sebastian laughed. "If I could find a cryptid, film it for my show? That would... well, I could retire happy. I mean. I wouldn't retire, but I could if I wanted to."

Basil chuckled. "Maybe we should have looked closer at Lake Taupo. See if there's a Nessie in there."

"More likely a taniwha. I bet there is one. Maybe more than one, it's such a big lake with lots of rivers feeding it."

They turned back without deciding to out loud. By the time they got back to the hotel they were able to get their room key.

The clerk looked past them to the gathering black clouds that were darkening the sky.

"Strange weather out there. Looks like you came in at the right time."

"The wind was getting chilly," Basil said. His nose itched and he rubbed it absently.

"Do storms like that blow in often?" Sebastian asked.

"Every now and then." The hotel clerk frowned and passed them their keys. "But nothing was forecast for today."

"Mm. Strange." Sebastian gave him a bright smile. "Thank you."

Their room was lush, Art Deco accents everywhere and a very comfortable bed. Basil stretched out on it and sighed, feeling out of sorts suddenly. He closed his eyes and realised what it was. The storm wasn't natural. It had a magical source.

"Bastian, the storm." Basil sat up on the bed, looking for his boyfriend.

Sebastian came out of the bathroom.

"What about it?"

"Someone's causing it, casting it, or perhaps summoning it?"

"Huh." Sebastian went to the window and looked out. "Why would someone summon a storm?"

Basil chewed on his lower lip, thinking. "Usually, well at least with the people I know, calling rain is just to water plants or to relieve a drought. But there hasn't been a drought, so … I have no idea."

"Maybe for the drama? It looks very Gothic horror novel." Sebastian went to his camera bag and pulled out his camera, filming the storm from the hotel window as it rolled over the ocean and then the town, bringing torrential rain with it.

"Well." Basil got up to look at the rain as well. "Let's not go out again until dinner?"

"Works for me." Sebastian filmed some more and then set his camera to charge.

CHAPTER SIXTEEN

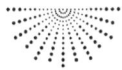

*S*ebastian's disquiet had returned with the storm.

He'd been feeling better since the walk, since thinking about the old Usborne books and what had gotten him into the whole ghost-chasing business in the first place, but the knowledge that now, for no apparent reason, someone was summoning a whole-ass storm brought the discomfort back.

He lay on the bed and distracted himself looking for a good place to eat for dinner, flicking through various options on his phone.

What am I doing? I need to record a piece to camera about turning into a cat. I need to do that while it's fresh in my memory.

And I should do an update about travelling to Napier as well.

But when he considered talking to camera about being a cat his stomach rolled unpleasantly, and his shoulders hunched up.

He hated feeling this way. He loved magic, he loved weird stuff. But being hit with a curse was an entirely different experience. He had never imagined anything like that happening to him, and now that it had... He was afraid.

Beside him, Basil was reading a novel and possibly dozing off.

Sebastian couldn't record his piece to camera with Basil listening. He'd have to admit how badly it had shaken him and he didn't want to worry Basil. He didn't want to imply that he was now afraid of Basil either. Or at least, of what Basil could be capable of.

Basil would never hurt him. He knew that. Without Basil he'd never have been turned back to human form. But a small, panicky part of his brain was still deeply afraid, as he had been as a cat. He couldn't forget that Basil had the same magical energy, the same potential to do something like that to him.

He took a deep breath and sighed it out, letting his phone fall as he laid his forearm over his eyes. Maybe if he could nap, he'd feel better afterwards?

Basil moved, followed by the sound of a book being put down on the bedside table. Then Basil slipped an arm under Sebastian's neck, wrapping his other arm tight around his waist, and resting his head on his chest.

The warmth of the gesture, and the gentle understanding and empathy that came with it, unlocked something Sebastian had been holding back. He began to cry.

He had no idea when the last time he'd cried had been. Sebastian was a natural optimist, something he loved about himself. But it also meant he didn't often give in to feelings of sadness or fear.

His silent weeping turned into something more shuddering.

"It's all right." Basil's voice was soft enough to ignore if Sebastian wanted to. "You're safe."

Sebastian gave in and let himself sob, grabbing a tissue from the bedside table and pressing it to his streaming eyes.

"I was so afraid." He choked the words out around the tightness in his throat. "It was everything I was. I was so small, every emotion overwhelmed me. I thought I'd be stuck..."

Basil hummed his sympathy, squeezing him, and listening.

"I'm so grateful to you. Thank you. But it's kinda shaken me as well. I feel differently about magic, and I hate it."

"That's perfectly understandable. You went through a traumatic experience, anyone would be afraid."

Basil's words loosened the knot in Sebastian's stomach and he breathed slightly more easily. He held Basil close, feeling the relief mingle with pure love as he squeezed his boyfriend.

The tears dried up as quickly as they came, and Sebastian sniffed, wiping his face and blowing his nose while Basil held him loosely.

"Are you all right?"

Sebastian tossed the used tissue into the bin and nodded. "I feel pretty drained, but I think that was good. I needed to let that out."

Basil rested his chin on the top of Sebastian's head and sighed. "Is it okay if I call you kitty sometimes? I don't know why, but it suits you."

Sebastian snorted against Basil's chest and laughed. "I guess it's okay."

"You really were an adorable cat, if that helps at all."

"I should watch the footage, and film my response to it, my experience." As he said it, Sebastian felt himself cringed away from the idea. Maybe one crying jag wasn't enough to heal the trauma.

"There's no rush." Basil stroked a hand down Sebastian's back. He remembered how perfectly comforting that had been when he was in cat form and tried to relax into it. "I know you like quick reactions to things, but you have to be mentally sturdy to do that, and I'm not sure you're quite there yet."

"I think you're right."

They both jumped as a crack of thunder boomed overhead. The lights in the hotel room flickered.

"That was close." Sebastian laughed, a little nervously.

"Really close," Basil echoed.

The lights went out altogether and after a second, the fire alarm started up. It was a loud whining drone that couldn't be ignored. They both scrambled off the bed. Sebastian grabbed his camera bag and stuffed his phone into his pocket, slipped on his shoes.

"You're not supposed to take anything with you when there's a fire alarm," Basil said.

Sebastian shrugged and reached for Basil's hand. Basil had grabbed the bag with his book of shadows inside it. They hurried out together, Sebastian grabbing the swipe card for the room on the way.

A handful of people were in the stairwell, but it didn't appear that the hotel was booked out. There was plenty of room to move down at a brisk pace that wasn't running, and no one jostled Sebastian.

Outside the staff had high-vis vests on and were directing people over the road to the grassy park where there was no shelter to be had. The rain was unforgiving, pouring straight down and flooding the gutters.

"This is ridiculous," Basil said. "We can't stand out here in the rain, we'll catch our death."

Sebastian looked around. Some people were moving back to the built up side of the road to shelter under awnings. Restaurants nearby were open.

"How about we go for an early dinner?" Sebastian suggested, pointing up the road at the place he'd read about online.

"Anything to get out of this rain."

Basil turned to head in that direction and collided with a tall man who turned. Like a recurring nightmare, Asher smirked down at him.

"You again? What are the chances?" He had his hand on Basil's arm, steadying him, tugging his jacket back into place. "I did think I saw you by the side of the road earlier today."

Sebastian felt a thrill of fear so powerful it transformed into anger. He pulled Basil back, away from the tall stranger.

"Please leave us alone," he said, through gritted teeth.

"No need to spit like a tomcat, I'm only saying hello." Asher's words, and his smarmy, condescending smile were utterly repulsive to Sebastian. The allusion to cats sent him into another stratosphere, and his hands curled into fists.

"What did you just say?"

"Now, now." Gently but firmly, Basil gripped Sebastian's arms and steered him away. "I don't know what you're doing, following us, but you'd best do what he said and leave us alone."

Sebastian's mind raced. He'd seen Asher the night before at dinner, he'd shaken his hand. And then he'd mysteriously turned into a cat.

Now Asher was here? Why was he here in Napier? Why had he been in Taupo? Why was he following them? Had he really turned Sebastian into a cat and then mocked him with it?

"Basil, we can't let him get away with it," Sebastian turned, trying to see Asher in the crowd. He was nowhere visible.

"There's so many people here." Basil's voice sounded shaken. "Whatever he's playing at, we can't start brawling with him in the middle of a crowd, in the rain. We'll get arrested."

Sebastian saw the reason in that and tried to quell his anger.

He saw the sign for the restaurant up ahead and led Basil to it.

The concierge met them at the door. "Oh dear, caught in the storm?"

"Yes," Basil said. "The hotel had a fire alarm and we weren't prepared. We don't have a reservation but could we please have a seat?"

"Of course. I'll find you some towels as well." They were directed to a table and in a moment the concierge returned with a couple of clean hand towels.

"That's so kind of you, thank you," Basil said.

Sebastian felt better once he was seated and dabbing himself dry with the towel. But the uneasy feeling that they had to deal with Asher remained.

"What are we going to do, Bas?"

Basil wiped his face with his towel and set it in his lap. "We're going to eat and then we're going to think it through."

Sebastian nodded, slightly unsatisfied with that answer, but not willing to argue about it.

CHAPTER SEVENTEEN

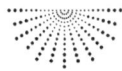

asil looked over the menu. The restaurant had a Māori
chef who was interested in integrating traditional
dishes with Western cuisine. They offered a degustation menu.
Usually Basil would have been very keen to order that but he
didn't feel quite right.

Whether it was the shock of the fire alarm and the cold rain,
or meeting Asher unexpectedly *again* he wasn't sure. Maybe he
was rattled from the night before, and from seeing how it had
upset Sebastian?

Whatever the reason, his stomach felt tight and he didn't think
he could manage eight courses.

The a la carte menu it was, then. He perused the options and
decided on something relatively simple, fish with a side salad.

Basil eyed the wine menu but a wave of nausea hit him at the
thought of it. He blinked, feeling faint.

"Are you all right?"

Sebastian looked concerned.

Basil took a deep breath and nodded. "Just feeling a little ill,
but I'm sure it will pass."

Sebastian's eyebrows drew together. "Asher touched you,
didn't he? Could he have cast a spell on you?"

Basil shook his head and regretted it, feeling dizzy again. "No, I'm certain I would have felt it if he'd…" He scanned his body, looking for something out of order. He did feel something. Not on his arm where Asher had touched him, but there was something else. He checked his pockets and found something small and hard in his jacket pocket. With a sinking feeling he withdrew it. A small, clear quartz crystal with a crack down the centre. "Oh fuck."

Sebastian reached for it but Basil closed his fingers around him, stopping him. Basil wished, as hard as he'd ever wished anything, that he was back home with his books, herb garden and all his supplies.

"No, don't touch it. This is bad luck. It's on me, and I'm sure he's done something to bond it to me, but if you don't touch it, you won't be affected by it."

Sebastian's jaw was working, clenching and unclenching as if he were fighting the urge to punch something.

"It's all right. I'll toss it in the sea." Basil took a breath. The nausea had passed but he still felt slightly light-headed. "But food first."

"If you're sure?"

"I'm sure. These kind people brought us towels and I want to eat to settle my stomach."

Dinner was exquisite. Basil was sorry he didn't have the appetite for the degustation as it was sure to be incredible. Maybe tomorrow after they'd sorted out this crystal and had a good night's rest?

In lieu of dessert they each had a hot chocolate, and once Sebastian had paid they ventured out again. The rain had eased to a light drizzle and from the lack of crowed outside the hotel the fire alarm situation had been resolved.

They crossed the road and went down the back towards the stone beach.

Basil summoned his magic as he approached the crashing darkness of the waves. Vague lessons from his mother popped up in his head. *Salt water cleanses crystals. If you let go of something it won't affect you any longer. Any negative energy cast into the world with magic returns to the caster sevenfold.*

If that last one was true, Basil may not need to do anything at all to Asher. The universe would punish him quickly enough.

But it didn't benefit anyone to sit still and wait for karma, not when he had a crystal that likely held a hex in it on his person.

With Basil's magic active he could feel the crystal itself. Heavy in his palm. An energy like a black hole, sucking at him, making him feel physically weak. He wrapped some of his own magic around it, forming a protective bubble to prevent it working, and took a deep breath. He centred his focus, pulled back and threw the crystal as hard as he could manage into the ocean.

His next breath felt clearer, more sustaining.

Behind him, Sebastian stood with his arms wrapped around himself.

Basil went to reassure him. "There, I put some of my own magic around it and now it's gone."

Sebastian adjusted his camera bag and slipped his arm through Basil's. "Let's get inside. It feels like the storm is coming back."

When Basil took off his jacket in the hotel room he felt a weight in the pocket. With a sinking stomach, he reached in and pulled out the crystal.

"He must have done a sticking spell on this." He sat on the bed and flipped open his book of shadows. He couldn't concentrate on the pages, the room felt like it was spinning. With a groan he pressed his hand to his forehead and closed his eyes.

"Are you okay? Can I help?"

Without opening his eyes Basil pushed the book towards Sebastian's voice. "Look for sticking spells. They keep a thing attached to a person, like this crystal is."

Basil's head throbbed, and he groaned. All he wanted to do was sleep.

"Maybe you should rest," Sebastian said. "I'll let you know when I find something."

"Thanks." Basil kicked off his shoes and wrapped the blanket around himself. He was no longer afraid or angry, he needed to sleep. He didn't fall asleep so much as he was dragged into it.

"Come find us!"

"We need you to find us, it has to be you…"

"Please!"

"Basil, Basil Robinson!Come and find us!"

Basil woke with a start, his head throbbing with… not pain, but urgency. He rushed to the bathroom with the vague notion he might be sick, but once he was in there he only needed to pee. He pressed his head against the tiled wall as he relieved himself and tried to make sense of the night.

He had woken from a dream in which multiple voices were calling to him, wanting his help. Before then he had been hexed or cursed by Asher, and he still had the token of the curse. He needed to … he needed to go.

The voices hadn't been just a dream. They were too real for that. He tried to summon visuals from the dream, put faces to names, but there was nothing more than shadows in his memory.

But he did have a road sign. In his dream he'd seen a sign that read '*Norsewood welcome*.' That was something.

He washed his hands and went back to bed. Checking the time, he saw it was three in the morning. He'd slept for hours. Sebastian was sitting up against the cushions, snoring, Basil's book of shadows in his lap. With care, Basil took the book from him, closed it and set it on his bedside table. He gently urged Sebastian to lie down fully and pulled the blanket up over his shoulders.

Basil settled back into bed beside him, but his skin felt too tight. He could feel every hair on his body and what's more, it felt as if the world was alive around him. *The universe itself is watching. The room is aware of me.*

Closing his eyes, Basil took a deep breath and tried to centre himself. If the universe was trying to tell him something, perhaps meditation would give him guidance on what to do, what the message was.

His hand closed around the cracked crystal. He had left it in his jacket, but now here it was in his palm. Of course it was.

Slowly, he got his breathing to a deep, regular pattern. He concentrated not on the awareness of the universe, which was far too unsettling a concept, and instead thought about the shape of his body. The physical form that existed around the purple well of magic, his mind, and his soul. He took his time, feeling his way mentally around each aspect of himself and checking in.

His body felt fine, no particular ache or tension that he needed to resolve. A small twinge in his jaw perhaps, that was easy enough to relax. Physically he was doing all right, which was a good change from the vertigo and nausea from earlier.

His soul? Well, how did you take stock of a soul? He sensed a disquiet within him, but that could be put down to the fact he had a cracked crystal in his hand, sent to him by someone who wished him harm.

Magic was the next thing to check in on. It was there, as it always had been. Dormant, but there. He felt its potential. If he tried to, he could summon it to his hands or his eyes. He could conjure something.

He nudged at it, more out of habit than from any desire to do anything magical. Usually his magic felt like warm water, flowing up his limbs in an instant. Akin to a tap being turned on.

Now it was more like trying to coax molasses. Slow to move, in need of heat to flow. But what heat could he possibly bring to his magic? It was responding, glowing as bright as usual, but something held it back.

He squeezed the crystal, feeling helpless. He wished he could shatter the damn thing and be free of it.

"Please! Someone help us!"

He didn't hear the voice with his ears, he could tell from the lack of movement or response from Sebastian. The words reverberated in his brain. He'd heard it though, resonating through his soul from somewhere beyond.

That was the sign, that was the message. The universe or his magic, or perhaps even the cursed crystal were telling him loud and clear.

They would have to go to Norsewood. There was no other option. Just where Norsewood was, he had no idea. But Basil would have to go there.

That decision made, he relaxed into the hotel mattress. Sleep took him in an instant.

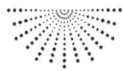

CHAPTER EIGHTEEN

*S*ebastian woke up, checked that he was still human-shaped, checked Basil for the same, and picked up his phone. He used the first hour of his day looking for interesting news and pings on the saved searches and news threads he had followed. He opened another tab for 'the breaking of curses' but there wasn't much information he felt could be trusted on the web.

The missing car full of teenagers was the top news story, although there was precious little for the news to report. He read interview with one of their parents.

Michael is described by his father as a sensible boy, with no history of misbehaviour or poor driving. "Michael, if you're out there, please come home." The Father's desperate plea is echoed by people all over the country who are hoping for the safe return of the teenagers.

Basil woke up and slapped the bedclothes with one hand.

"Norsewood!" he croaked.

Sebastian snorted. "Good morning to you too, love of my life."

"No, I mean, yes good morning. But I had dreams and visions, and well, I heard voices. Someone's missing, or lost or in danger, they need our help. We have to go and find them."

"In Norsewood?"

"Yes." Basil sat up and ran a hand through his tousled hair. "It was very clear in my vision that I need to be there, and I heard people begging for help. They sounded so afraid, Bastian. They said my name. Something is happening, something big, and the universe wants my attention on it."

Sebastian's heart thudded, and he swallowed another jokey reply. He'd never seen Basil like this. His eyes were wide and flustered, and he was already scrambling out of bed. Sebastian pulled him back by his arm.

"Basil. How are you feeling?"

"All right." Basil rubbed his own forehead and nodded vaguely. "Not actually well, but the room isn't spinning and I don't feel nauseous."

"Okay. Let's grab some breakfast and head to Norsewood."

"Where is Norsewood?"

Sebastian pulled up his map app on his phone and found Norsewood. "An hour twenty. Not far at all."

Basil huffed out his breath. "Is it okay to do this? I know we were thinking we'd go to the aquarium today?"

Sebastian took Basil's hand and squeezed it. "It's totally fine. The aquarium will still be there when we get back. If you had an otherworldly message about someone who needs your help, we need to listen, right? I'll film it if there's anything to film and we'll sort it out. Maybe it's tied to the curse or whatever as well, right?"

Basil's tense jaw relaxed slightly. "Right, yes. Good."

They got up, dressed and were down in the hotel dining room within twenty minutes. They snagged some muffins and fruit and went right to the car instead of sitting down to make use of the breakfast buffet.

They both brought one bag each, leaving the rest in the hotel room. Basil's contained his book of shadows and magical equipment, Sebastian's was his main camera, and the backup batteries.

Sebastian was driving out of Napier in no time. He put on one of his chillout playlists and tried to ignore the knot in his stomach.

Basil ate two blueberry muffins and fell asleep.

To say that Sebastian was worried about Basil was an understatement. He had been terrified that he'd wake up to find a fluffy white cat beside him in bed. The relief that Basil had still been Basil was immense. But they weren't out of the woods by any stretch of the imagination.

Basil was feeling better but he clearly wasn't a hundred per cent.Hopefully whatever happened in Norsewood, would solve the entire situation.

He hoped and hoped.

If I had magic of my own, I could lift a curse. I could blast Asher in the face. I could ... Well, I could do so much that I can't do now. But if all I can do is get Basil to the place he has to be, that will be enough.

Basil woke up just as they approached the tiny township of Norsewood. Multiple signs heralded the town as a proud purveyor of woollen goods. Sebastian had been inclined to let Basil sleep until they pulled in, but Basil startled awake.

"You okay?" Sebastian spared him a glance as he checked his mirrors.

"I felt something." Basil peered out the window. "Magic. A field, or a warning, a barrier spell. Not dissimilar to the wards I put on the house."

Sebastian frowned, trying to puzzle that out. "The town has a ward?" He flicked the indicators on and slowed for the turn into Norsewood. There was no one else on the road, so they didn't have to wait. The approach to Norsewood was a steep road through a patch of dense pine forest, a sharp contrast to the flat farmlands on all sides.

A quaint wooden sign read *Norsewood Welcome* and had an axe as a decoration. A symbol hung from the sign, a weathered wooden circle with a square cut out of the middle, bisected with two lines forming an X. Did it mean something or was merely decoration?

"That's it." Basil's voice was strained. "That's the sign I saw. That exact one."

Sebastian was torn between excitement for the hot trail of a new mystery, and absolutely terrified about the power of the magic at work.

As they drove up the road the village centre was revealed on a small hill. It consisted of Victorian-era weatherboard buildings, the largest one being the inn, a handsome white-painted two-winged building with a sign proclaiming it *"Norsewood Crown Tavern."* An information centre, a small town square, and a selection of shops and a dairy with a petrol pump out the front of it completed the town.

There was no one in sight.

Sebastian shivered. The drive down had been pleasantly warm, and he'd had sunshine on his arms, but as soon as they'd turned into Norsewood they were under thick clouds. The temperature had dropped several degrees.

Basil scanned their surroundings. "This isn't right. There's something amiss here."

Sebastian pulled into one of the many empty car parks in front of the information centre.

"Maybe you'll get a better feel for it if we walk around."

They stretched their legs, studying the town. Sebastian grabbed his jacket from the back seat and slipped it on. Basil looked pale and Sebastian tossed him the sweater he'd brought as well.

They made their way into the information centre. The woman behind the desk was probably in her sixties, and she looked tired out. Her name tag said 'Kathy'.

"Good morning, Kathy." Sebastian put on his warmest smile and approached her desk. "How are you?"

"Fine." Kathy eyed them both with deep suspicion. "How can I help?"

Sebastian looked back at Basil, but he was frowning at the map of the area.

"Right, well, this is going to sound strange, but I'm actually a professional on strange." Sebastian handed her one of his business cards. "I have a YouTube channel about ghosts and strange occurrences, and so on. I wanted to know if anything particularly weird or unusual had happened here in Norsewood, lately?"

Kathy snorted, looking at his card, flipping it over and shaking her head. "You're kidding me. You're a professional ghost hunter? And you're here because you think something strange might be happening?"

Sebastian was used to this kind of response to his introduction and had a regular response. "That's right. I know it's probably not what you expected to hear this morning."

"Ridiculous." Kathy stood up. "It's exactly what I expected. Come with me, back outside."

Basil took Sebastian's arm as they followed Kathy back out of the information centre and to a nearby white picket fence that surrounded what looked like a café or restaurant. There was a plaque attached to the fence that read *Three Happy Trolls*.

Kathy motioned to the fence. "Here's the first thing. Our trolls have gone."

Basil frowned. "Trolls."

"S'right." Kathy stared at the fence with an almost repulsed expression.

Sebastian noted the long pieces of timber on the ground in front of the fence. There were changes in the discoloration of them, as if something was usually positioned on top of them. Three things.

"The three lucky trolls protect our town. They're carved of wood, although some say they simply chose to take that form. They've been here longer than I have, and they have names and everything. They keep the village safe, and well, the night before last they vanished."

"The night before last…" Basil leaned more heavily on Sebastian.

"Did anyone see anything?" Sebastian asked.

"Nope, but it's pretty quiet here in the evenings," Kathy said. "Store closes at six. Mostly people are at home by then, minding their own business. Not a big drinking night at the pub. And this is after the disappearances of the tourists as well."

"Tourists?" Basil piped up.

"That's right, four or five teens on a road trip, their car and all, gone. Then there was a group from China who came through on a mini-bus on a special tour, spent up large at the knitwear store, but two of them never returned to their bus."

"I'd heard news about the teens, but I hadn't heard about the tourist bus," Sebastian said.

"Well, they're not reporting that one, are they? Looks bad for tourism if people just don't come back to their bus." Kathy sighed deeply. "I don't know what to tell you, boys. The police aren't finding anything and they've all but given up. Strange is something we're used to here, with our Norse heritage and the Viking boat and all its ghosts, the little trolls in the bushes move around and no one thinks anything of it. But these three, they're always at their posts. It's shocking to see them gone like this. No one feels safe."

So many things I want to know more about. Where do I even start?

"How big are these trolls?" Sebastian imagined something small, doll-size things perhaps.

Kathy held her hand up at shoulder height. "Around that. And solid timber, heavy things. Not easily lifted and stuffed under a jacket if that's what you're thinking."

"Bastian, I feel faint," Basil said.

Sebastian slipped his arm around Basil and guided him to the nearest park bench.

Kathy frowned and followed them.

"What's wrong with him?"

"I'm cursed." Basil leaned forward and put his face between his knees. Sebastian felt filled with renewed motivation to get to the bottom of it all.

"Thank you Kathy. My number's on my card if you hear anything or think of anything else that may be of use. I'm going to settle Basil and then do some filming around the village. It sometimes turns up useful things."

Kathy gave a single bob of the head, walked back into the information centre without another word.

Sebastian rubbed Basil's back. "Stay sitting, okay. Do you want anything? A drink or a snack?"

Basil nodded yes and then groaned. "The vertigo. Maybe one of those sports drinks might help."

Sebastian hurried to the dairy and got a chilled bottle of something blue that promised to have electrolytes in it, and a chocolate bar. He carried them all to the counter, where a sallow-faced man eyed him. His shoulders slumped, and his checked shirt looked as if it was from the fifties, it was so threadbare and faded.

"Good morning, just these thanks." Sebastian flashed him a smile.

The man eyed his selection and held out a hand.

"Oh, uh, right." Sebastian pulled out a twenty and placed it in his palm.

The man took the money, hit a button on the till and gave him a handful of coins as change. Then he settled back into his slumped-shoulder position. His eyes never left Sebastian.

"Thanks, I'll just…" Sebastian gathered the purchases into his arms. "Thanks."

As he left the shop he glanced back. The shopkeeper's eyes were still on him, large and expressionless. Sebastian shivered and closed the door firmly behind him.

"Shopkeeper didn't even speak." He handed the bottle to Basil and set the chocolate beside him. "It was like he was walking dead or something. I'm going to get my camera and walk around, film some stuff okay? You stay put. Call out if you need anything, I won't be far."

Basil shakily sat up and took a deep swig. "Yeah. Thanks."

Sebastian went to the car and pulled out his camera. He chose a spot in front of a tree and did a piece to camera, selfie-style.

"Hey, we're in Norsewood, which was an unexpected leg of our journey. Here's what I know so far. First, Basil was woken in the night with visions of people calling for help, and a street sign that said Norsewood. So, here we are. Five teens vanished from somewhere around here a few days ago, with their car and everything, never made it to their next destination, last seen here." He sighed and looked away. "What else? There's a magic forcefield or something that Basil felt when we drove in. He's not in too good a place, it seems to be affecting him physically."

Sebastian swallowed the lump in his throat. He wanted to protect Basil so badly, but how was he supposed to do that when he didn't even know magic?

He looked back at the camera. "What's more, we just spoke to the woman at the info centre, and she said there are two tourists who didn't return to their tour bus when it was stopped nearby. Also the village's three lucky trolls, which are carved out of wood, vanished in the night. Something really intense is going on here… Oh, that's the other thing. Basil's been cursed. We think we know who did it, but breaking the curse is a puzzle we haven't solved. My gut feeling is that this is all linked, so. I'm gonna film some of the sights and hope that I work something out as a result."

He hit the stop button and lowered the camera, fighting the urge to hug himself and maybe cry a bit.

He couldn't sense the magic but knowing that it was there put him on edge. He loved mysteries, he loved uncovering the truth, but this particular day it all felt like too much.

He sighed, positioned the camera on his shoulder and walked slowly around the village. A Viking longboat rested in a glass case. Next to it was a modest paved square, and in every patch of public garden, he spotted small trolls. The villagers must be fond of finding ceramic, clay and wooden trolls and leaving them to be discovered. Seeing their little faces was deeply unsettling. Surprises each place he looked. He found himself imagining that they could come alive at any moment and run away giggling.

"What am I going to do?" Sebastian asked himself.

He looked back towards the bench he'd left Basil. At least he was sitting up now, looking brighter as he sipped the sports drink.

Sebastian walked back to him.

"I'm feeling a bit better." Basil gave Sebastian a tight smile that didn't reach his eyes. "I expect the curse is interacting with the ward and I'm taking the toll of that."

Sebastian grimaced. "Ugh, that sounds horrible. Let's try and get this solved as soon as possible, then."

Basil nodded and then winced, his hand going to his forehead.

Behind him, Sebastian heard the crunch of footsteps. It sounded deafening in the quiet of the near-empty village. He turned, expecting to see Kathy but instead it was Asher Montgomery. He looked taller, less gaunt, and infinitely more full of malice.

"Took you two long enough. Good morning Basil."

Sebastian moved so his body was in between Asher and Basil.

He put his camera on his shoulder and started recording. "What have you done?"

Asher looked at the camera with amusement and rolled his eyes.

"How is Basil feeling? Not too well, I'd expect. It's a nasty little thing, the draining spell. I can't imagine how awful…" He moved closer.

Panic rose in Sebastian, thundering his heart and quickening his breath. He held his ground though. He couldn't let this man, whatever he was, get to Basil.

"You turned me into a cat."

Asher smiled wider, a rictus grin that shot another bolt of fear through Sebastian. "I did. You non-magic types can be so resistant to magic sometimes, you have to use the simplest path. For you, that was a cat. Did you enjoy it? Tell me how much you hated it, I'd love to hear."

Sebastian's jaw tightened. He didn't want to say anything about being a cat. He might give Asher more power with his despair and horror of it. What was he doing? He couldn't fight a witch, or a demon or whatever Asher was.

"What do you want with us?" he demanded.

"Us?" Asher let out a deep laugh. "My dear boy, you were supposed to be a tool, something to give me power for the ritual. I wanted him." He pointed directly at Basil. "He has power, and I need it. Simple really. I just need you to get out of my way."

"That's never going to happen." Sebastian reset his stance. "I won't let you touch him."

"Ah, little tomcat," Asher taunted. "You should have been a good boy and run away in fear like I intended. You'd have been so much easier to sacrifice in that form." He raised a hand and electricity crackled between his fingers. Above them the clouds grew darker, more threatening.

Sebastian's heart skipped a beat, processing all of that. "You want to sacrifice me?"

Asher smirked. "Catch on fast, don't you, puss-puss?"

Sebastian was about to punch Asher, magic be damned, he even fisted his hand.

"Hold on." Behind him, Basil spoke up. His voice was stronger than it had been a moment before. There was the sound of movement. Sebastian didn't dare take his eyes off Asher to check.

"Why do you want power?"

Asher's smile eased into something more human. "Same reason anyone does. I want my magic to flourish."

Basil touched Sebastian's elbow. He dared to glance at him then, and was relieved to see he had some of his colour back, and was standing steadily.

Basil glanced nervously at Sebastian.

"But magic doesn't work like that, Asher. Magic is like a tree, it needs water, light, and other trees around it to truly flourish. It needs community."

Asher scoffed. "Trees don't need other trees."

"They can grow alone, that's true enough, but to flourish they need others. Trees pass information between them, they even, some species, leave space between the edge of their own branches and the next, so that each leaf gets sunshine. They call it being crown-shy." Basil had the air of a professor, dispensing knowledge.

Sebastian's mind whirled, trying to see a way out of this situation that didn't end up with Basil or himself being hurt.

Basil stepped towards Asher, away from Sebastian's side.

CHAPTER NINETEEN

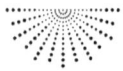

*B*asil's knees were unsteady. He was grateful that he was on the paved road and not the gravel path, because he might well have fallen over. But he was certain in his gambit. If Asher wanted his power to grow, the way to do it was with community. It had worked for Basil, and the other witches in his little community group. His parents lived near dozens of witches on Waiheke. Covens were a thing for a reason.

"Asher, I can offer you a community. A number of very lovely witches gather at my library, and we'd be happy for another member to join. We all have power, and we're happy to share what we know, lend our efforts to spells and such like."

Although every atom in his body shouted at him not to, Basil stuck out his hand to shake in a gesture of peace.

"Interesting proposition," Asher said. His expression was utterly blank and unreadable. "Show me the crystal, would you?"

Basil fetched it out of his pocket and held it out on a flat palm. Was Asher going to take it back? He desperately hoped so. It would be wonderful if all this stress could be resolved with a genuine offer of friendship.

Asher placed his hand palm down over Basil's, pressing the

crystal between their hands as he closed his long fingers around Basil's in a death grip.

"So obliging. I appreciate your attempt to reach out, I do, but it's so much easier for me to simply take what I want."

Searing pain tore through Basil. Stronger than any pain he'd felt in his life. His knees buckled and he slumped to the ground, although Asher's grip kept him from falling all the way. He was left on his knees as Asher forcibly sucked magic out of him, using the crystal as a conduit.

Basil screamed. He wanted to look for Sebastian but his eyes wouldn't open. His ears roared with static and he clawed with his free hand at Asher's wrist, trying in vain to get free.

"That's it, let it out, let me have it all," Asher crooned as if to a baby. "This will be done very soon and then you can go back to your library and your boyfriend and forget that you were ever a witch, you'll be so content."

Basil's eyes flew open. Asher intended to take all his magic?

He could feel the purple well inside him draining, the energy flowing from deep within, up his arm and into Asher.

He had to stop him, but how?

"No!" The pain intensified again, leaving him whimpering.

"Those children, the moment in the cave, the cat spell, the trolls, all of it was to get your attention, Basil. To get a taste of your energy. You have more power than you ever use. You glow with it, and you're content with salt circles and petty wards? I will make far better use of your magic than you ever could. I will live forever."

Basil whimpered, trying to pull his magic back but it was futile, trying to change the flow of a rushing river.

"If you hadn't been so slow to catch on, I could have—"

What Asher could have done went unsaid.

Basil fell back to the road with a painful crack to the head, and the pain vanished. He looked up, confused, and saw

Sebastian's car. Asher was some metres away, sprawled on the ground.

Sebastian leaned out the window. "Get in!"

Basil's limbs felt stiff and sore, but he propelled himself up and into the passenger seat. "Did you just hit him with your car?"

Sebastian put the car into reverse and shot back towards the road they'd driven in on, away from Asher who was slowly picking himself up.

"It was the only way I could think of to get him to let go of you." Sebastian's eyes were bright, he reached for Basil's hand. "Are you all right? What was he doing?"

"Sapping my magic." Basil squeezed Sebastian's hand then lifted it to his mouth to kiss the back of it. "Thank you, that was brilliant."

Sebastian smiled but his eyes were still wide. "What do we do now?'

Basil bit his lip. He focused on his magic. It was still there. Depleted, that was for sure, but it was still there.

"I don't know. He said he wanted to use my power to… to live forever."

On the other side of the village Asher slowly picked himself up.

"I could hit him with my car again?" Sebastian suggested. He sounded quite keen to do it.

Basil couldn't blame him.

"I don't think that will stop him. I need time to think." Basil leaned forward, put his head on the dashboard and closed his eyes.

Focus on my breathing. In and out, where can you feel it? Lungs, diaphragm, nose, mouth. It fills me with life-giving air. Find the quiet in my mind, it's always there behind the panic. Think of nothingness. The source of my magic…

Wait. Basil sat up. What was the source of his magic?

He'd always thought of it as the fourth aspect of his body.

Body, mind, soul and magic. Could you actually remove someone's magic? Asher thought you could. It might kill the victim, or it might leave them as he'd suggested, an ordinary person. People lost their minds and continued to live. People lost use of their bodies and could live on as well. What about the soul?

Basil shook his aching head. No time to philosophise. The important question was what was the source of his magic. It was depleted but if he could just access a little more...

Asher walked towards them.

Sebastian turned the car and drove down to the main highway. "He'll follow but it will give us a bit more time."

Basil closed his eyes again. "Thank you."

He breathed. He looked into the darkness within himself. All the books he'd read on magic, all the teachings he'd had, all the advice from his parents... he'd never read anything about where magic actually came from, besides *some people have it and some don't*.

Which meant what? He sucked his breath in through his teeth. The car juddered over a rough country road and came to a stop. Basil ignored it. Sebastian could keep Asher at a distance, he didn't need to worry about that.

Beside him, Sebastian started talking, and Basil recognised it as his 'to camera' voice. Was he livestreaming? Perhaps asking for help?

It didn't matter. Basil thought again. Trolls. Teens. A transformation spell. A leeching spell. Asher wanted to live forever. Five teens, two tourists...

He had to stop him. The offer of friendship had been thoroughly rejected. He had to go on the offensive. He had his book of shadows, a handful of crystals, and some half-used candles. Not enough for a ritual... And what kind of ritual could be possibly do? A binding to stop Asher hurting others? A shield to lock him out?

A combination of the two maybe.

Basil breathed deeper, slowing his heart rate.

He'd offered Asher the thing he truly believed in. Community could help. He didn't have a community here. Or did he?

His eyes flew open and he looked at Sebastian, who was talking rapidly into the camera, explaining the situation.

"Ask everyone to focus their attention." Basil shuffled closer, leaning in to see his own face on the screen next to Sebastian's. "Sorry to interrupt, but all of you watching can help us. Magic is about focus and will, that's what my mother reminded me of recently. In this case it's only the two of us against a powerful witch who is focused on draining my magic. He has a lot of willpower, and it hurt when he touched me. I don't have the supplies to do a big spell, something that would compensate for it being just me with magic, and we certainly don't have the time."

Sebastian slipped his arm around Basil.

Basil was vaguely aware of how cold his hand was. He paused to give him a quick kiss on the cheek. "Sebastian has bought us time but it's not enough for a ritual. However, if all of you watching…" His eyes scanned the phone but he couldn't take in any information. Comments were shooting up from the bottom of the screen and there were too many icons to make sense of. "How many are watching, Bastian?"

"A few thousand." Sebastian pointed to the number of watchers with one of the fingers he was holding his phone with. "Everyone, this is better with more numbers, so please share this feed, put it on your social media, and if there's anyone in your house who could help, go get them. The more people the better."

"Exactly." Basil took a breath. "need everyone watching to focus on me and think about my magic. Think of it as a body of water, something large, a lake, a rushing waterfall after a winter melt, or a crashing ocean wave. Something powerful that you'd maybe be cautious about stepping into. It's purple, my magic, knowing that might help, I don't know."

Basil swallowed. "My mother said the actual objects required for a magic spell aren't as important as the idea of them so—"

The car rocked to the side as if a giant was trying to lift it.

Sebastian slipped his arm back from around Basil, slapped his phone on the magnetic dash mount and pressed his foot on the accelerator.

Basil twisted to see Asher behind them. His magic was a curious brown colour with a purple sheen, like oil in the sun. His rictus grin was back and he had both hands raised, glowing with magic.

Sebastian pulled onto the highway.

"We have to go back to Norsewood proper," Basil was as sure of this as anything he'd ever been although he couldn't have explained why. "By the trolls, where they are supposed to be. There's power there, the belief of the community."

"Right." The tyres screeched as Sebastian hauled on the wheel and took them back up the hill.

"Strange that he didn't try and get into the car," Basil said. He was mostly thinking out loud. "But you did hit him with it… Perhaps your love, your belief in your car, the connection you have to it acted as a sort of barrier?"

"I do love to drive." Sebastian's tone was off-hand.

Basil leaned in to look at the phone. Comments scrolled faster than he could keep track of. The view counter had shot up to 30,000 people watching. That was good. Even their attention on them would count for something, energy wise.

"We have to keep streaming this, Bastian. I need their eyes on me while I attempt this."

"Gotcha."

Sebastian pulled up outside the Norsewood info centre and grabbed the phone. Basil hopped out, going straight for the plaque with the happy trolls. He had his book of shadows in hand and without looking, flipped through it and opened it to a random page.

The book didn't disappoint. He looked over the page to see it was titled *Severance and Binding.*

"Perfect." Sebastian was standing a few feet away, filming with the phone. Basil gestured him closer. "My book has come up with the perfect spell, film it so everyone can read, the more everyone knows about this the more they can help."

He held the book and checked in on himself. His magic energy was growing. His heart swelled. Maybe this would really work?

He scanned the page and saw the list of requirements and focused on willing the idea of them there. Green candles at each cardinal point. The ashes from a family's cooking fire. Fresh plucked sage flowers and bristles from a witch's broom. All familiar items, but none that he had to hand. But that didn't matter. As his mother had said, it was the energy you needed.

He pulled on his restocked source of magic and gestured, sketching a circle around them, pointing to each direction and imagining the items appearing as he did.

The smell of burned wood, faint scents of rosemary and beef from a stew.

The softness of the purple sage flowers, their scent prickling his nose, so familiar to him from his garden back home.

The witch's broom, a proper besom made from a gnarled branch with thick bristles, slim and whippy.

"You're too late for all of that," Asher said. He was close.

Basil whipped his head to the side and saw him.

Asher stood outside the imaginary circle that Basil had cast, which was a good sign. He held the cracked crystal up and chanted some words.

He's counter-casting. I hope he's not stronger than me.

Basil closed his eyes and refused his will. He had thousands of people rooting for him, pouring their intention into him, he could feel it. He had cast the circle, he had summoned the items he needed and now he just had to read the magic words.

He opened his eyes and called all the magic in him to his throat. When he spoke his words crackled with magic.

"Asher, by the power of the winds and the earth below us you may not tap magic from me or any other creature. Not witch, not fairy, not human. Nothing. Your power will be your own and no more."

Asher made to speak but no sound left his open mouth. He pressed his hands to his throat, staring at Basil with wide, disbelieving eyes.

The words he spoke weren't exactly what was on the page, but as Basil scanned them they flowed and changed, matching more closely to what he needed. He sent out a silent thanks to the book and to the universe itself for aiding him.

"Your access to my power is hereby severed, and will never be renewed. You will no longer feed on others to fuel yourself. This severance is permanent, so is the ban on you. You will do no harm to others, Asher, I hereby bind you by the power of the broom and ashes. So it is."

The magic poured out of Basil as he said the final three words and he saw it wrap around Asher like a mystical scarf before it vanished. Asher sagged and then fell to the ground in a heap.

The power of the circle, which Basil had been aware of in the back of his consciousness ebbed and ended. Basil took a quick breath.

He turned to Sebastian, who was aiming his camera at Basil, and the other camera at Asher. It should have been an awkward stance, but Sebastian seemed totally at ease, and he was beaming ear to ear.

"Thank you everyone who helped!" Basil said to the camera. "I could feel the power of your focus. Thank you. I couldn't have done it without you." He caught movement in the corner of his eye.

"Did you fix it?" Kathy was watching from the door to the info centre. "I was helping too."

Basil took a deep breath. "I believe so." He sent his awareness out, casting a wider net. The strange barrier that had affected him when they first drove in was gone. He felt the soft nudges of a new energy nearby. "Yes. It has. I think the trolls are going to come back on their own."

"What about him?" Kathy gestured at Asher laying on the ground.

"Is he dead?" Sebastian asked.

"Shouldn't be, but he might have aged a lot all at once." Basil stepped out of the fading magical circle and approached Asher's form. He used his magic to send out tentative feelers to check his body over. Yes, there was a pulse, but it was weaker than Basil would have liked.

Asher let out a soft moan as Basil got closer. "What did you do to me?"

Basil crouched beside him, letting some of his magic flow into Asher's body, easing the pain he detected. His face looked older, certainly, more lined and weathered. His hair had more grey in it but he hadn't aged to what Basil expected his true age to be. "I stopped you from sapping energy from others, that's all."

Asher groaned and sat up, his head almost colliding with Basil's. "You really think that will stop me?"

Before Basil could answer Asher laughed. Lightning flashed down from the sky and struck him. When Basil's sight cleared from the dazzle, he was gone.

CHAPTER TWENTY

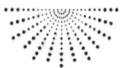

"*I*'m as much a fan of a dramatic exit as anyone but that was over the top." Sebastian stopped filming and slipped the camera into its bag. Then he thanked the crowd watching the livestream, promised to update them all later and cut the stream.

Basil had fallen back on the road when the lightning struck, and Sebastian hurried forward to help him up. "Are you okay?"

"Yes, I think so?" Basil held tight to Sebastian's arm as he helped him up. "My head is clearer." He let go of Sebastian and checked his pockets. "The crystal is gone."

"Good." Sebastian wrapped his arms around Basil and held him tight, letting all the fear and adrenaline wash over him now that the threat was gone.

Finally Basil pulled away and they both turned to Kathy. The person from the dairy had come out to watch as well as a few more people.

The clouds above them cleared and the sun shone down, warming Sebastian's shoulders.

A car pulled up beside Sebastian's, a white corolla filled with teenagers. All five of them piled out.

"You would not *believe* what happened to us," the driver said.

He had red hair and mid-brown skin. "It feels like I've been driving in circles for hours, this endless loop that we couldn't pull off of."

"Yeah, I thought Mikey was faking it, but we couldn't even pull over to switch drivers. We were meant to be in Napier ages ago."

The girl stretched her arms over her head. "And there was no signal on any of our phones. Couldn't even text."

"You've been missing for several days," Kathy said.

A brutal way to break the news. Sebastian stepped forward to show his phone screen to the teens.

"I assume you're this group that the news has been reporting on? Michael, Enid, Ana, Joseph and Melissa? We're really glad to see you, there's been some really intense magic happening and it looks like you got caught up in it."

One of the girls peered at the phone and let out a whoop. "We're famous?"

"I gotta call my mother," Mikey said.

"And we should let the police know," Basil said.

Kathy slapped Sebastian and then Basil on the back. "I'll call the cops. You'll have to stay the night, enjoy some Norsewood hospitality."

Sebastian yearned to say yes, but he remembered how flustered Basil got when plans changed. They hadn't even brought a change of clothes with them. All their things were in Napier. "That's very kind of you, but we should really—" he began.

Basil cut in.

"That sounds like a lot of fun, thank you. Is there somewhere I could have a nap before dinner? I'm somewhat wiped out."

"Of course." Kathy introduced them to Barry, who ran the Crown Tavern. Then she made a surprised noise. They looked in the direction she was to see two confused looking Chinese tourists walking up the road.

Barry showed them directly to one of the rooms.

"Room thirteen. It's not much, but it's clean," he said. "And no charge, assuming the trolls come back like you said they would."

Basil laughed and nodded. "Oh they'll be back, I felt them."

"Right. If you need anything I'll be downstairs at the bar."

Sebastian shut the door and turned to Basil. "You surprised me, I thought you'd want to stick to the plan and head back to Napier."

Basil removed his shoes and flopped backwards onto the bed with a happy sigh. "Well, Napier isn't far. We can head back in the morning, there'll still be plenty of time to see the aquarium."

Sebastian set his camera and his phone on to charge. "You're right, I thought—"

"I'm so relieved that I'm not cursed any more that the idea of changing plans doesn't bother me at all. The plan was already pretty well messed up, and besides we'll still get to do all the things we want to, right?"

"Of course."

"As long as I'm with you, I know I'll be safe, and that well, evil witches with dark motivations aside, we'll have a good time."

Sebastian set his shoes beside Basil's inside the door. He heard voices in the hall and smiled. Barry and the teenagers, they must be taking some rooms as well.

"I'm very glad to hear it."

"Now, come here kitty, cuddle me while I fall asleep."

Sebastian had conflicted thoughts about the pet name, but Basil using it like that was very different to when Asher threw it in his face. He climbed up on the bed beside Basil and wrapped his arms around him. "If you insist."

Basil nuzzled under Sebastian's chin. "Brilliant thinking, with the livestream by the way."

Sebastian chuckled. "I may not have magic, but I do have followers on social media."

"It really helped. I don't think it would have worked at all without them."

"You were amazing, today." Sebastian squeezed Basil closer and kissed the top of his head. "Your magic is so strong, you astound me."

"Are you still afraid of magic?" Basil asked, after a moment. His voice was softer now.

Sebastian closed his eyes and examined his inner self. "No, I don't think so. Maybe a little, but I'm not afraid of you. I have a healthy respect for magic now."

"Probably for the best." Basil yawned and closed his eyes.

Sebastian made a mental list of things to do later. He'd do his piece to camera, the reaction for being turned into a cat. He was still afraid to, but his viewers deserved to see the truth, and if that meant the emotional truth of it as well, Sebastian would give it to him. He'd also like to film the trolls once they returned. See if Kathy, Barry and the others would give him interviews about the trolls and what else they'd noticed around town. Then he could also interview the teens and get their story. There was a lot of good material there, and he'd get several videos out of it, or one big, long one.

For now, though, all he had to do was hold his strange, magical and slightly-less-anxious boyfriend. He closed his eyes and breathed in the familiar fresh-herb scent of him.

Basilwas breathing softly, so deep and regular that it lulled Sebastian to sleep as well.

CHAPTER TWENTY-ONE

*W*hen Basil and Sebastian made their way downstairs, hours later, the sun had begun to set. Basil became aware of the noise of a crowd.

Norsewood wasn't a big town, by anyone's description. It was a farming community with a few central amenities, but apparently everyone from the surrounding area had come out tonight.

The pub/restaurant of the Norsewood Crown Tavern was all polished wood and a wide bar, several tables had been pushed together to host a veritable feast. Large platters of food filled the table. People lined the sides. Barry carried a tray of beers to those waiting to eat. Maybe fifty people?

In the crowd, Basil spotted Kathy, the Chinese tourists and the teenagers. There were two empty seats beside each other, halfway down the table.

"There they are!" Barry called out.

Everyone turned to look at Basil and Sebastian.

Basil thought again of the Lord of the Rings and the birthday party the hobbits had for Bilbo. Although that was at the start of the book and not after all the adventures, knowing hobbits they'd probably have feasted at the end as well. He raised his hand to wave, feeling oddly like he ought to make a speech although he had no idea what to say.

Sebastian laughed outright. "Is this all for us? You shouldn't have, this is amazing! Thank you!"

Kathy jumped up from her seat to usher them to their places. "Oh hush. It's not that much. Everyone brought something. We all agreed we owed you some thanks for sorting things out around here."

Barry was next. Tray under his arm, he shook both their hands as they were moved towards the table. "What would you like to drink? Anything we got, on the house."

"That's very kind. Uh, white wine would be perfect." Basil shook out his hand as subtly as he could after Barry's enthusiastic shake.

"One of those pints looks good," Sebastian said.

Kathy sat them down in the middle of everything. Barry delivered their drinks and took his place at the head of the table. He raised his own cup of beer and cleared his throat. "To Basil, to Sebastian and to the return of our trolls!"

"Here, here!"

"Cheers!"

Around the table glasses were clinked together. Basil tried to tap his glass on every one that was offered to him, but with the stretch of the table it wasn't possible to get everyone.

"So the trolls are back?"

"That's right." A young woman wearing a Swandri nodded. "No one saw it, but one moment there was nothing there, the next, they were back."

"Hah, I thought they'd wait until dark…" Basil stored that mystery away as something to ponder when there wasn't a feast in front of him.

Someone said grace over the food and then people started to dig in.

How someone had found the time to roast a leg of lamb

while he slept, Basil had no idea, but he was grateful for it. The meat was seasoned with generous amounts of garlic and rosemary and smelled heavenly. Sebastian passed him a gravy boat, then the Swandri woman passed a basket of rolls. Basil's plate was soon piled high, and his rumbling stomach demanded to be fed.

"This is incredible." Sebastian thanked the people sitting nearest them. "We didn't expect anything like this."

They shook their heads, and made shooing gestures with their hands. "It's nothing."

"Eat up."

So they did.

Halfway through, when Basil was taking a little wine break, Sebastian turned to him, beaming, with gravy on his chin. "Not bad for a little place, huh?"

Basil took a deep breath and let it out as he considered his answer, and his next morsel of food. When they'd hit the road, days ago, he'd thought they had an air-tight plan to stick to. That they would be visiting Waitomo and Napier and maybe stopping one or two places on the way. That he'd be eating food at expensive restaurants and sight-seeing in between naps and catching up on his reading.

Instead they'd encountered benevolent ghosts, a vicious witch bent on immortality, they'd both been cursed in different ways and Basil had improvised with his magic. They'd caused the rescue and return of seven missing people, and three missing trolls.

It was not what he'd expected, and he hadn't enjoyed every second, but right in that moment, he felt utterly at peace with the world.

"It's wonderful," Basil said. He dabbed the gravy off Sebastian's chin. "I'm having the best holiday ever. I can't wait to see what tomorrow will bring."

He kissed him warmly to cement the feeling of contentment

and all around them the residents of Norsewood whooped and clapped.

If you enjoyed this story, please consider leaving a review on your preferred book platform. I am planning at least two more adventures for Basil and Sebastian and your warm words are excellent motivation.

GLOSSARY OF TERMS

Car boot - also known as a trunk, the part of the car where you put your luggage

Plonked - set down without ceremony

Pā - a fortified village used by a Maori tribe

Te Reo - the Maori language

Tane - a name, meaning the god of the forests, pronounced Tah-nay

Karakia - a blessing or prayer chanted out loud, to invoke guidance and protection for those listening

Hongi - a traditional and warm Maori greeting which involves clasping hands as in a handshake and pressing noses together

Tapu - sacred or taboo

Ngaire - a name meaning flax flower, pronounced similar to Nigh-ree

Iwi - a tribe, a grouping of tribes, loosely used to mean the tribes of a particular area. Plural form is the same as singular

Moko/ Ta Moko - a facial tattoo, sacred

Korowai - a flax cape adorned with feathers and tassels

EFTPOS - a point of sales system that can take regular bank cards as well as credit and debit cards, and the main method of payment in New Zealand

Ruru - a native owl

Dairy - kiwi name for a convenience store, dairies are usually locally owned, and stock all sorts of necessities including candy, chocolate and hand-rolled ice cream

Swandri - a brand of woolen coat, usually patterned with red and black checks and seen on almost every farmer in the country

ALSO BY JAMIE SANDS

OVERDUES AND OCCULTISM

Buy now

A witch in the broom closet probably shouldn't be so interested in
a ghost hunter, right?

That Basil is a librarian comes as no surprise to his Mt Eden
community. That he's a witch? Yeah. That might raise more than
a few eyebrows.

When Sebastian, a paranormal investigator filming a web series
starts snooping around Basil's library, he stirs up more than just
Basil's heart.

Between Basil's own self-doubt, a ghost who steals books and
Sebastian, an enthusiastic extrovert bent on uncovering secrets,
Basil's life is about to get a lot more complicated.

Overdues and Occultism is a sweet, no heat contemporary novella
about a witch living in Auckland, New Zealand. MM romance,
HEA.

ALSO BY JAMIE SANDS

MONSTERS AND MANUSCRIPTS

Buy now

One Witch

One Paranormal Investigator

Something that went bump in the night...

Library witch Basil and YouTuber Sebastian have settled into life together in the sleepy suburb of Mt Eden.

Basil is overjoyed to have a handsome boyfriend to come home to and he is connecting deeper with his magic. But when strange books start to turn up at his library and an uninvited guest makes noises in their attic, it's up to them to investigate.

As a paranormal YouTuber, Sebastian can't resist a new mystery. Especially since he's been in one place for far too long... Is his enthusiasm for the next story going to ruin everything?

ALSO BY JAMIE SANDS

THE SUBURBAN BOOK OF THE DEAD

Buy now

No one expected the last night of the Summer holidays to be deadly.

Rain and her best friends Rachel and Jackie head to the carnival. Rain's plan was to chat up Jake, who runs the Ferris Wheel, and maybe get a kiss or two.

But Rachel is killed in mysterious circumstances, and none of them will ever be the same again.

When Rachel returns as a ghost insisting Rain find out who killed her and why, she turns to Jake, who knows more than he seems to. In fact, he's encountered weird stuff like ghosts and monsters before. So now she just has to grieve for a friend who she's still talking to, try not to fall deeper in love with Jake, keep her family off her back, decide who to trust, infiltrate the funfair and find Rachel's killer. Piece of cake, right?

This book has been re-released with a new cover and back matter from the 2018 edition

There are three golden rules for new recruits at Fairyland Theme Park:

1. No breaking character, even if you're dying of heat exhaustion
    2. Always give guests the most magical time
    3. No falling in love.

Nate's only been at work one day, and he's already broken all three.

Fast-tracked into a Prince role, Nate's at odds with Dash, the handsome not-so-charming prince who is supposed to be training him. Nate doesn't know how he ended up on Dash's bad side, but the broody prince sure is hot when he gets mad.

Dash has worked long and hard to play Prince Justice at Fairyland. Now, instead of focusing on his own performance, he is forced to train newbie Nate to be the perfect prince. Nate's annoying ease with the guests coupled with his charm and good looks could dethrone Dash from his number one spot … so why does he secretly want to kiss him?

Fairyland heats up as sparks fly between the two rival princes. Will they get their fairytale romance before they're kicked out of Fairyland for good?

Find out in this standalone MM contemporary romance by Jaxon Knight, set in an amusement park where fairytales can come true.